MORE THAN JUST A SKIN

Memoirs of Eve

Eve Naomi

Cover Design by:

Digikube Media
(digikubemedia.com)

For information on distribution, translation or bulk sales,
Please contact:
evenaomi42@yahoo.com

Dedication

To God who created me.
To Grandma who raised me.
To my daughter and all young girls who need to be inspired.

Disclaimer

This is a memoir — a true life story. However, all the names have been intentionally used to replace the original ones. Any resemblance to actual persons, living or dead, or actual events is purely coincidental.

Table of Contents

Introduction

Even from my mother's womb, I knew that the world was not going to be friendly to me.

That sounds a little strange, right? Yeah, I agree that it does. Yet, in even stranger ways, I was sure that was going to be the case for me.

I knew that the world was going to deal with me in ways that I could never forget. I knew that I was going to be served a barrage of complicated life situations that were going to be etched forever in my memory and in my history.

Maybe I should have just stuck in there - my mother's womb, I mean - but hey, I had to get out so she could go about her business. Hahaha...

So I got out. And into the unfriendly world that dramatically shaped these experiences which I am about to share with you in this book.

Yes, I know that there are a million and one stories that you've been told before; or that you have heard already or even listened to.

Stay with me, okay? My story has an interesting twist to it and I am pretty sure that it would do one of five things: inspire, encourage, push, strengthen or empower you. Or maybe you would experience all five of them; which would be great, wouldn't it?

My aim is to touch your life in very positive ways, as I know that we all carry our peculiar burdens and scars with us. If we are lucky, we find those who have had similar experiences and we can learn from them. If we are unlucky, we get to wallow in our pain and live miserably, forever.

I am one of those people you want to learn from their life experiences.
Oh, I know you'd like to know what it is that makes my story different. Yeah? So
what if I told you that all my life ordeals were bordered around the skin?

Ah! I caught a big chunk of your attention right there, didn't I? Hahaha...

"What is it about the skin that has pushed you to write a whole book about it?
I hear you ask.

"How could your story possibly change me?" You wonder.

Stay with me.

****

The skin is the first thing people notice about you. Not that they go out of their
way to do so; it's just that your skin kind of precedes you. Before you open your
mouth to say anything, your skin goes ahead to introduce you.

Before people even get to know who you are or what you have to offer, they meet
your skin first and, believe it or not, this influences how they treat you.

People look at your skin first before they look into your eyes to have a glimpse
of who you really are. Before they see your welcoming smile, they biasly assess
your skin first. Before they feel the warmth you possess in your whole being,
they scrutinize your skin. And before they experience the love you have to share
from within you, they make their decision based on the colour of your skin! Isn't
that rather rash?

Now mind you, I'm not talking about mere complexion here. I am talking about
the way our skins place us at different levels of importance and prominence in

the world. What I'm talking about here is skin-deep. It is deeper than hereditary - whether genes or DNA. It goes beyond family health history or medical factors.

I am talking about the whole essence of who we are. I am talking about the human race. I am talking about us - all of us - and how we have deviated from the original plan of divinity for humanity, to carve a painful path for ourselves. A path which has pierced very deeply into our psyche and emotional fabrics.

Why are some people seen as superior over others? Why has supremacy become such a painful and misconstrued reality, reminding us that there is such an unfair advantage in the world? Why have we misinterpreted supremacy?

Again, I know these are probably some of the questions you have heard before or even asked yourself a thousand times over. But we never really get our answers, do we?

The truth is that those questions will continue to linger and persist until we have found some sort of succour. Which is relative because we all hurt in different ways, and so what serves as an adequate answer for one might just be merely scratching the surface for another. However, what we have in common here is, the *pain*. We crave closure as we strive every single day to answer those nagging questions which tug at our very existence.

I am sharing my experiences because I know it will resonate with you in some ways; I know that a piece of my story will be life-changing for you. I am certain that some parts of my story will make you smile, chuckle or perhaps shed one or two tears and then laugh through it. You know why? That's because those will be tears of victory, tears of renewed strength, tears of determination, and tears of validation.

No, I'm not writing to remind you of those pains; I'm writing to inspire you. I am writing to set you on that spring that would launch you forward and get you going, no matter what you have been through. I am writing to teach you to look past the hurt and pain, because way beyond them is a stronger you!

Okay, enough already of these talks, hahaha. Let's get this ball rolling already, shall we?

****

Chapter
1

Then, There Was Eve!

See that thing called fate? It's a fascinating concept. It's like the wind that blows about and doesn't give a clue as to when or where it would settle.

While we are at liberty to choose whether to establish a relationship with the people we meet, we are totally helpless when it comes to deciding **who** those people are. Ah, fate decides that for us! Just like the wind, it blows us about and then settles us with whomever it pleases. Perhaps, that's the only time the skin really doesn't matter. Dare I say that fate surpasses all and doesn't discriminate when it comes to skin? You bet I do!

That would be the only reason my parents came together. And the only reason I came into existence – fate - because both of my parents were from different ends of the world; from totally diverse continents. More about them shortly. I would like to linger a bit more on the general effects that our skins have on our existence.

So fate brought me into the world. But could it shield me from the cruelty, meanness and hatred that I was going to face just because my skin was different? Sadly not!

I mentioned just a while ago that my parents came from the far ends of the world; one from the African continent and the other from the European continent. It should be an exciting thing to be **made** from two whole entities, shouldn't it?

Well, not for me.

My dual identity turned out to be hellish - the most excruciating pain one could ever experience.

In retrospect, I wonder how I survived all the ordeals I went through. Could I say it was because of my strong-willed trait? Well, maybe. Or did my infectious humour have anything to do with me surviving the loads of cruelty that were thrown at me? Perhaps, it had to do with me being a helpless romantic? Hahaha.

Whichever of these factors was the reason I survived the things I have survived in my life, I am very grateful. I can't tell you how thankful I am to God for keeping me alive to be able to write my story and share it with the world.

Yes, that's it! It's divinity! That's what kept me all those endless and horrible years! God was always there to protect and preserve me.

But of course I could never have been able to bear the pain if I didn't have the love and backing of my maternal family. They were loving, caring and highly supportive. Don't worry, you'll meet them soon, hahaha.

Before then, suffice it to say that despite being from diverse cultures and the hellish effects that it brought with it, my mother's family was able to love me adequately. Each person showed me that they deeply cared for me, in their own ways.

While I suffered severe psychological damages from the world at large, my mother's family was my support. I could count on them anytime! Otherwise, I couldn't have survived one bit!

More Than Just A Skin - Memoirs of Eve

Chapter
2

Meet Eve

Just like many other babies, I was born to two adults - my mother and my father. But unlike other babies, I did not grow up with my parents because they were never together as a couple — I told you it was just fate that brought them together in Europe to **make** me. Thereafter, dad had to go back to Africa and mum had to work; she was still such a young girl... which left me with Grandma and Grandpa; my mum's parents.

I was born with a dark skin. My undoing!

Here's why...

Remember I told you that my mother was from the European continent? And that my dad had to go back to Africa? Which left me with my mum's parents? Yup! I was raised in Europe, surrounded by white skins! Everywhere! Now close your eyes for a moment and imagine how I felt in their midst...

Exactly! Out of place!

It was bad enough already for me, being the only black skin around. But boy! Did they make it obvious and rub it in, every chance they got! They made me feel like a substance and not a human being. How dared I pollute their precious and sacred environment with my black skin?

Can you imagine what it felt like to be constantly talked about — every single moment I was breathing and walking around? Hey, I'm not talking about being talked about in a celebratory kind of way... I wish!

But I was the object of hateful talk; people talked about me in disgust, like they could close their eyes and wish me away from their environment that I had desecrated with my skin colour.

School was one place I had to go to and from, every day; but of course it was another opportunity for people to talk down at me and remind me of how different I was from them. Imagine going to school in the morning and returning later in the day, and constantly being talked about! The psychological damage this did to me!

With time though, the hatred started to make me strong. You know why? I had to survive it; I had to device a coping mechanism for myself. It was either that or die from the torture and constant cruelty. So I started to grow **thick skin**. Ironical, isn't it? This same skin that was my source of sorrow also taught me how to be strong and how to survive.

Now, this was me and how people's cruelty and insensitivity affected me. How about the effect it had on my family? Oh, sure it did affect them! Deeply too! My suffering was their pain. My torture wrung their hearts. My tears tore them apart.

And the worst thing was that they could not do much to alleviate my pain. No matter how much they tried or how much comfort they managed to give me, the outside world was determined to make my life miserable. All my family could do was to continue to love me - unconditionally. Did I mention that this was what kept me going? Oh, it was! Plus the **thick skin** I had grown, hahaha.

Hey, what was it that they said about clouds again? Oh, yeah! That every cloud has a silver lining? Well, I'd say this is true.

Yes, in the midst of the hatred, cruelty and torture, there was some level of positivity. How, you ask?

Well, while some hated me and my skin and wished me dead, some did find it fascinating. Some people actually admired my dark skin and thought I was cute. Imagine the relief for me, hahaha. A breather for Eve! All thanks to silver lining! And as you read on, you would see how this silver lining kept saving me!

Moving on...

My hair was afro and no, that's not because it was how I was born or that was how I liked it. My poor grandma did not just know how to take care of my hair. If she did, it had the potential to be very long and even get all the way to my waist – which was my dream!

A girl could dream, couldn't she?

Alright, let's forget for a moment the reality my skin had forced me into...deep within me, I was a dreamer. Not in a 'wishing-I-had-what-I-couldn't-have' kind of way. But I had mental pictures of what I could look like if I was allowed to manifest all my girl-charm. Hahaha. I fantasized about flinging my hair unconsciously from my face and swooping it up in a bun sometimes.

Anyway, back to my afro hair.

Instead of taking me to beauty salons to make my hair, my grandma always had it cut and this made me look like a boy – one more reason for my haters to torture me. In this case, I really didn't blame the haters because even I didn't like the short, afro hair myself. As a matter of fact, I hated it! More especially that it was a routine – I had to go to the barbing salon, mostly on Saturdays, to have my hair cut. Gosh! Interestingly though, I chose to have it cut on Saturdays so that by Monday – when I had to go to school – hopefully it would have grown a bit longer, hahaha! Told you I was a dreamer!

Bodily, I was slim. And while this was a perfect stature in Europe and for my maternal family, for my African family on the other hand, I would have appeared to be sick! See my dilemma? Hahaha.

Africa is a beautiful and interesting continent, you know. They believe that one of the ways one can show that they are healthy is to flaunt it – on their bodies. Simply put, if you are slim, it means you are sick or malnourished. In Africa, healthy living means being full-bodied. This would explain why my father thought I was sick when I finally met him. More about our meeting later.

I learnt that in some parts of Africa, young women actually go to live in what is referred to as fattening houses, where they are fed excessively, in readiness for their husbands. The fatter they appear, the healthier it shows that they are; and the more appealing they become for their husbands-to be.

Whereas, on this other side of the world, if I dared add weight unnecessarily, I would be considered unhealthy! Interesting, isn't it? Beliefs! Cultures!

As little and insignificant some of these factors were, they affected me greatly. Was I supposed to be fat or slim? Was I supposed to be fair-skinned or dark-skinned? Was I supposed to grow my hair long as a girl, or not? Which language was I supposed to speak?

What was I supposed to think of my father, whom I never really knew, growing up? And my mother who had to leave me to go and work? Was I supposed to understand that as a child? Why did I have to visit the barbing salon, and not a beauty salon? I was – actually **am** – a girl, a female, for crying out loud!
I had a million questions and zero answers!

More Than Just A Skin - Memoirs of Eve

So many times, I had to ask God, "Why me?" I needed Him to help me answer some of those questions. I wished He could help explain some things to me. I prayed that He lessened some of those burdens that weighed down on me. So I asked, "Why me?"

Perhaps, if He explained to me why He chose me to bear those pains, I would understand with Him and maybe, just maybe, it would have helped me to bear the pains in a more accepting manner.

But I didn't have those answers. And so the pains continued, excruciatingly!

Chapter
3

True Face of Racism - The Reality

People are just plain cruel!

If you haven't really experienced racism, you would only have a surface understanding of what it really is. You would only grasp as much as words can describe; the reality of it remains to be experienced first-hand; to be felt directly.

This said, I certainly do not wish that anyone should go through it! It is not an experience you want to have. Ever! Trust me on this.

It was one thing to be constantly reminded of how different my skin was and how less of a human being that made me; at least according to their beliefs. And then it was another thing to hear them call me those horrible names!

"Black thing on the floor!"

First let it sink in that I wasn't only crucified here for being black or having a black skin; I was also referred to as **a thing**! An object! And on the floor!

While that is sinking in, I want to remind you that every single name (word) I was called had its purpose and deep meaning.

I wasn't just a black-skinned person. I wasn't just a thing, an object. But I was **on the floor!** Indicating how inferior they thought I was. They seized every opportunity to establish their white supremacy! They were **up** there and I was

down there! Has that sunk in now?

"Asphalt!"

That's right, they called me an asphalt. Again let's look at that on a deeper level.

An asphalt is dark, to begin with. Secondly, it is mixed with sand and gravel. Thirdly, it is used as a road surface. Are you catching on yet? Yup! The road is where people walk on and where vehicles ply on. Note again how this implies inferiority and displays the supremacy power-play.

The road serves people; it is used by people. And an asphalt is just one of the ingredients used to make roads. See how insignificant they felt I was? Oh, it wasn't just a feeling, they made sure I understood it and that it sank in. What better way to establish that than to call me an asphalt? Like they were telling me, "Get that right!"

"Dirty thing!"

I was constantly reminded of how unclean I was; just because of my dark skin. I was reminded of how much I polluted their environment. They rubbed it in how undeserving I was to mingle with them. I was simply a dirty thing. Again, I was being referred to as an object – thing!

"Dead thing!"

While others were kind enough to refer to me as 'dirty,' others thought otherwise; worse! They thought I was dead! How could a dirty, black thing be a living thing? No way! I was dead to them. Not a living organism.

So how would you treat a dead thing? I leave that to your imagination.

"Monkey!"

We all know how very closely monkeys resemble human beings. They behave like them, can almost walk like them, eat like them, and so many other areas of similarities. The only difference here is that monkeys are NOT human beings!

So when someone called you a monkey, especially if you were a person of colour, it simply meant that you were regarded as sub-human! It meant you were less than a human being.

"Black people smell!"

This one hurt in a different way, you know. Whenever they taunted me with this, it felt like I was carrying the burden and sin of the whole African continent on my shoulder! I was an African descent and since I was the only one around in my environment, I had to bear the full brunt of our crime! Crime of being black!

Imagine being called all these names. On a daily basis! Every single chance they got! I wasn't spared at all. Can you just picture how this made me feel? Can you visualize the psychological damage it did to me? The truth is that I grew up hearing those names in my head and in my subconscious. They stuck with me!

Now you should know that I do love my African heritage and origin; honestly, I wouldn't change that for anything. But you should also know that sometimes it was very confusing, and rather frustrating for me, as a growing child.

Was I Black or was I White?

When you're Black, you're Black.
When you're White, you're White.
But when you're mixed race, you find yourself in the middle! In a mixed culture!

And what you face is the huge problem of fitting in!

This dilemma was very obvious and crucial for me, especially in my teenage years. I mean, I was still trying to find myself and deal with all the complications that come with being a teenager. My teenage years was when I needed, more than anything in the world, some sort of validation. I needed acceptance – to be shown that I really mattered and that I was valued.
And yet, instead of this reassurance, I was constantly put down! Being called all those derogatory and demeaning names! Do you know how dangerous this was?

If it was not for God, I could easily have derailed. Lost it! Became something else! Maybe committed suicide! Who knows! But God always stepped in! Silver lining?

Remember I told you I had to grow a thick skin? Yes, I did. And that helped me to handle the crisis and the constant battles that welled up within me all the time. In the end, I ended up *just being me*. It was simpler *to be me* than anything else, really.

Having said that, let me get partial a little bit. Can I?

I might have grown up with Whites and maybe I am White inside, but if I had to fight for either the Whites or the Blacks, I would certainly fight for my Black people! Yup! Told you I was going to be biased a bit here, didn't I? Well, there it is!

I do have that strong attachment and natural pull towards my African origin. They are just such a beautiful people. They have beautiful souls and large hearts. You could rely on them and relax around them because they are very loyal people. Black is beautiful.

Chapter

4

Growing Up...

Amidst the turbulence, torture and cruelty, I grew up. Some days, it was so bad I felt like disappearing from the face of the earth. But other days, it was manageable.

I already mentioned that my maternal family was so loving and caring. I could never exchange them for any other set of people in the world!

Grandmother

Grandmother was simply an angel, ever caring and always there, loving me every single second!

She was of medium height and oh, so beautiful! When I looked at her, all I saw was beauty and the peace that she exuded. All I wanted was to be with her. Where I wanted to be was beside her.

Most of my clothes were created by Grandmother's own talented and loving hands. She took her time and crocheted my dresses and I wore them so proudly. I think biblical Joseph and I had a thing or two in common, didn't we? He had his own coat of many colours and I had my own hand-made dresses. The common thing was that we both wore our clothing very proudly. Grandmother invested energy and love to make my dresses and I had to give the value for it.

Another thing I loved that grandmother did was that she dressed me up as a dolly! Which made me feel like a girly and like a princess. Remember those fantasies I had about how I really wanted to look and feel? Well, grandmother made this a reality for me. I really loved it when she made me look like a dolly! Bless her heart!

Grandmother created memorable routines for the two of us. She would take me to the park to play and of course, she was there to protect me from any harm – which included name calling.

The icing on the cake of my relationship with me and my grandmother was when she adopted me. You mean how? Or why? Well. Remember that my mother had to go work and was never really there? Yes, since grandmother practically brought me up, at some point, she (and grandfather) had to officially adopt me.

Grandfather
I was my grandfather's pretty angel and cute, little princess. He did his own part by being supportive and protective.

He was tall – but then, what did height have to do with anything? All I needed from them was the love they showered me with, hahaha.

Grandfather always bought me things on his way back from work; you could imagine that I always looked forward to those moments. Some people would say he spoilt me but all I saw was love; my grandfather loved me deeply and had to show me in some ways. So what if one of those ways was to buy me things? A grandfather could buy his little angel gifts, couldn't he? Hahaha.

Sadly though, my shower of gifts ceased when I was 12 years old because this was when grandfather passed on. Need I tell you how painful this loss was? We were very close and so the pain was very deep! Another pain I had to bear!

But life kept rolling by. I had to move on, right?

Mother

Yes, she had to go to work after my birth because she was still very young. But with time, she got involved with another man – remember that she and my African father weren't really a couple.

The truth was that she had to move on with her life, part of which was getting married to this guy she got involved with.

Unfortunately, mother's husband didn't quite accept me. Another rejection, right? You bet! But fortunately for me, I was already used to living and being accepted by grandmother and grandfather. They were enough for me.

In fairness to my mother though, she found it quite difficult to deal with her husband not accepting me, her daughter. But hey, she had to show her loyalty to her husband, didn't she? She had committed to him and vowed to be submissive. Seeing me was actually very challenging for her – as she had to stay committed to her new family – and saw me whenever she really could.

Thank goodness I had my grandparents! What would have become of me! However, my mother's husband changed positively towards me much later.

Cousins

Growing up, I had four cousins – who were all boys! I was the, 'One girl standing!' Hahaha! Well, up until I turned 15, which was when my sister was born. We were very close.

Then there was another addition to the family much later; another cousin – a girl – was born when I turned 19.

Amongst all my cousins, I have to mention that I was closest to one of my aunt's sons. We really bonded and shared more together. He was so cool and I did enjoy what we shared together as family.

Altogether, we had fun and memorable moments as kids.

Aunts
I can talk about two of my aunties who were significant in my growing up. I'm not sure actually, whether there were other aunties. I do remember these two vividly and I know that they made an impact in my life as I grew up.

So there was this aunty of mine whom I visited frequently and actually spent my holidays at her place. I spent so much time in her place that I did make a friend or two in her neighbourhood. One of these friends would turn out to be my husband as you would see shortly.

As for my other aunt, it was really just a case of speaking more with her about things generally; she was helpful and very caring. I did eventually grow close affinity with one of her sons, my cousin, as I mentioned earlier.

Neighbours
One of my neighbours stands out in terms of the memories I have of her. She was a doctor; so nice and kind to me.

As a matter of fact, she took care of me to the point at which she wanted to adopt me officially. But my grandparents wouldn't let me go anywhere! Their little angel! Hahaha.

But I do remember this guardian angel of a neighbour and the impact her kindness had on me, till this day!

Then there were two other neighbours of mine – two ladies – with whom I became very close and even still in touch or contact with, up till this day! That's right!

Chapter
5

Preschool

One of the most fun periods of childhood is supposed to be between the ages of zero to five, isn't it? This was when children were meant to play hard, laugh hard, make friends, explore, discover their likes and dislikes, ask tons of questions out of their curiosity and basically – be children – carefree, free-spirited, laid back, enjoy life and all that it had in stock.

But I was not 'every' child, remember? I was different. Or so the world had come to make me believe.

My first experience of school was my pre-school, which I started at the age of six. Why not earlier? Maybe grandma was trying to get me grow a little more mature and stronger? Maybe she was unconsciously trying to shield me from the hostile world.

Did that really matter though? Did it help? Did it make any difference? I'd say, "Maybe not," because when I did start school, I didn't like it one bit!

****

It was like any other morning but I knew there was something odd about it.

Grandma had woken me up as usual, with her loving hugs and kisses. We had our habitual chit chat about how I slept, if I had any dreams, what it was about, what I wanted to eat for breakfast, and so on.

One of the odd things I realised was that she had woken me up a bit earlier than normal. The routine was that she let me sleep late, a bit into the late hours of the morning. By the time she woke me up, the house was already alive and busy as she would have gotten up to do some chores.

However, this particular morning, as she woke me up, I couldn't help but notice that the house still seemed a bit quiet. Grandpa was not even up yet, or he would have come in to plant a good morning kiss on my forehead.

Another odd thing was that grandma was talking in a low tone. Like she didn't want to make so much noise. I noticed all this and couldn't help asking.

"Grandma?"
"Yes, my sunshine."
"Why are you talking so low? Are you tired?"
She looked into my eyes and smiled broadly. But I could see something else there – weariness.
"No, my child. I'm not tired, just being careful not wake grandpa up yet."
"And why is he not up yet? He hasn't come to kiss me good morning."
"Well..." she started explaining, scooping me into her laps and holding me so close. "...you see, Eve, today is a special day."
"Special day? Why?" My six-year old inquisitive mouth asked immediately.
"You are going to school today."
"School? Why"
"Don't you want to learn?"
"Learn what, grandma? You teach me everything!" I instantly felt bad about this whole school thing. A kind of premonition overtook me and I just didn't feel good about it.
"Of course I teach you, my sunshine. But there are so many other things you need to learn that can only be taught in schools."
"I don't want to go!" Was my simple but firm response. I must have raised my

voice a notch high because then, grandpa walked into the room. I must have woken him up.

"Eve darling," He started saying, coming to plant my good morning kiss on my forehead. Alright, at least, we still had that in place. "You need to go to school to learn about the world, and all the things you would need to know in order to make money as an adult."

Now they were really confusing me! What exactly was it that I needed to go to school to learn? That I couldn't learn at home from grandma and grandpa? Or were they tired of me? No! Not at all! Certainly not! Grandma and grandpa loved me deeply and wouldn't let me out of their sight if they didn't have to! They couldn't be tired of me!

So there must be a very good reason for them wanting me to go to school. Still, it didn't make me feel any better. I just didn't want to go anywhere. Not to school. Not anywhere! I just want to stay with them at home. In peace!

But they knew better, didn't they?

The rest of the morning sort of went on silently. Grandma got me ready, gave me breakfast and packed my lunch box. It just kept feeling like I was being sent away from them!
Grandpa got ready too and when we had all finished, two of them took me to school – to my preschool.

Immediately we got into the school premises, I started crying. The whole premonition feeling enveloped me once again and I felt such deep sense of sadness. As I started crying, I stopped in my track and both grandma and grandpa had to stop too to try to coax me into getting along.

"Come on, child." My grandpa persuaded.

"It won't be as bad as you think, sunshine." Grandma encouraged.

"I don't want to go!" I wailed. Sadly. Which my grandma must have felt because I saw tears rolling down her cheeks and she didn't even bother to hide or wipe them away. She was sad too. Which made me wonder why they were insisting I go.

When I managed to look away from my grandparents to visually take in my school environment, all I saw was hostility. I saw pairs of unfriendly eyes staring right through my soul. The hatred that emanated from their glances pierced deeply into the fabric of my being. I felt right away that I didn't belong here! Even as a six year old!

Needless to say that I was miserable on my first day in school. And my source of misery wasn't the same as other children would have. For other kids, they could be sad on their first day because they missed their parents; they could be sad because it was a new environment or they could be sad because it was a new experience.

Mine was all that. And more!

I was sad within because I knew I was out of place. Odd. The other children looked at me uninvitingly. I could see no welcome in their countenance. For the teachers, they did their best to hide their disappointment – after all, they had to be professional because of the sensitive nature of their job. They were supposed to be accommodating and inclusive. And yet, beyond that, I could tell that they viewed me as different. Which I was, actually! And also the reason I wanted to leave! I didn't want to be in school! Simple!

After a few days, as my misery and incessant cry persisted, my grandparents had to go see the Head Teacher. They were really worried and wondered if I was going to encounter problems in school.

Apparently, the Head Teacher must have convinced them that I was going to be alright. He must have gone on and on about how some children had a hard time adjusting, especially at the initial periods of their schooling. Sure he would have assured them that I was going to adjust quickly and blend in.

It was easy for the Head Teacher to convince my grandparents but was it also that simple to erase the distaste other children had for me? Sadly not! I was still the one who suffered the hostility and aversion.

Contrary to what everybody thought – namely, that the other children were soon going to warm up to me – they never did. Surprisingly though, I didn't have any problem blending in. The problem was with the other kids.

Sure I adjusted but the adjustment was in the way I interacted with the other children. I avoided mingling so much with them; rather, I preferred to play alone. And as long as I did this, things were okay. The few times I dared to mingle and play with the other children, I got backlashes. I remember one of them vividly.

It was break time on a cool Wednesday morning. The boys were busy climbing on almost everything, running around, chasing each other and playing detectives by catching the bad guys and play-shooting them with their hands.

The girls enjoyed gentler and more hands-on activities. Like building sand castles. It was amazing how even from a young age, boys and girls started displaying these tendencies that characterized their genders. While the boys loved to be in motion and exert their energy, the girls were more reserved in their choice of activities. They were gentler and engaged in activities that got them thinking critically and where they had to display their creative inclinations.

Anyway, back to this fateful day.

I sat alone as usual, watching the other kids play. I was sitting on a bench in the play area, playing with my favourite doll – grandma had let me take it to school and my teachers had allowed it too. Thank goodness!

But as I watched the girls work together to build a giant sand castle, something stirred in me. I suddenly felt the urge to join them – the sand castle was coming up fast and it was so interesting to watch how the girls cooperated, working in unison to make sure their project worked. The natural social yearning in me was awakened. I wanted to belong. I wanted to be part of what they were doing. I wanted to feel an accomplishment.

So I dropped my doll on the bench and walked excitedly to the sand area: "Can I join you?" I asked timidly. Part of me expected to be turned down but the other part of me was very hopeful. Well, the hopeful part won!

"Sure!" They chorused. Did I hear right?

Before they could realise what they had done and change their minds, I quickly scooted down and joined the building construction. Hahaha.

"Put it here!"
"Keep your hand in place!"
"Be careful!"
"Let's cover this hole."
The girls chorused excitedly as the sand castle gained weight and grew in height.

Then out of the blues...

"Your hands are dirty!" One of the girls exclaimed. That's right, you're not mistaken! She was referring to me! You could imagine that all the building hands were white, except for a pair. Mine!

That comment got me! It pierced through my heart and slashed through my soul. It felt like I had been hit physically. And you would have thought that the other girls would condemn that comment. Alas! They joined in...

"Oh, that's true!"
"Why are they dirty?"
"Go wash your hands!"
"How come they are not like ours?"

I'd had enough!

Getting up as swiftly as I'd gone down to join them, I dashed back to the bench, picked up my doll and ran into the classroom. Where I went to a corner and cried my eyes out.
And the misery continued after that day. Things didn't get any better. I remember that all my school photos had me appearing odd all the time. I was always the different one – **that black girl with the black hair**. There was always, always one issue or another. My preschool sucked!

****

At age 8 anyway, I had a life-changing experience.

Since I couldn't be the kid I actually was while I was in preschool, the only other place to act out childishly was in church, hahaha. At least this was where I could play with some friends; just being carefree and free-spirited.

It was a Catholic church.

And if you are a Catholic or know someone who is, you would know that they are big on moral standards. No compromise, hahaha. As a kid, I used to see those religious leaders as being above sins; it felt like they were spotless and never even uttered any negative words, what with the white robes they wore. It made them look like saints. There was absolutely no way one could afford not to hold them in reverence.

It wasn't compulsory to belong to any church departments or activities, but I joined anyway — I was in the kids group. That afforded me the opportunity to mingle and make friends. Generally speaking, boys helped priests especially during mass.

On this particular day, after mass, I was on the corridor with some of my friends. We were laughing, shouting and chasing each other on the corridor, basically disturbing the peace and quiet of the environment. To us then, we were just a bunch of kids, playing and having fun.

But looking back now, I can say for sure that we were misbehaving, at least according to the high moral standards and expectations of the Catholic Church. At this point, the Priest was passing by and had seen our ill-behaviour. Of course, he wasn't going to spare us. Or more like, he wasn't going to spare me!

For whatever reason, the Priest singled me out to talk to me. Maybe because my friends saw him before me and had tactfully toned down their misconduct. Or maybe because that day was just the day God had orchestrated that my life would take a positive turn regarding my behaviour.

"Do you think what you are doing is acceptable?" He scolded me, pointing his stern, disciplining fingers at me. "You are a girl; a Christian girl for that matter! A lot is expected of you."

I could only nod in agreement; I dared not answer back. That was rude and disrespectful. I could not even maintain eye contact with him.

"I know that there is a lot of potential in you and I will not allow you derail from God's plan for you." He continued.

In my mind, I was wondering what God's plan had got to do with me playing with my friends and having fun. Was it a crime to have fun?

And as if he could hear my thoughts, he continued. "I know you think you are just playing but I must remind you that there are certain moral standards you should hold yourself up to."

I nodded, still looking down.

"You don't want to become irresponsible when you grow up, do you?"

I shook my head. Of course not. None of us playing that afternoon on the corridor had the intention of becoming irresponsible. But apparently, that was where we got it wrong. If we were not checked, and in a timely manner, our behaviour could escalate and revolve into sheer juvenile delinquency

"I expect so much from you. Let me not see you again in this kind of behaviour Not in church, not in your house, not in school. Not anywhere!"

I nodded again.

"Now run along!" He finished dismissively. And as I scuttled away, after muttering a shy thank you, I could still feel his gaze following me. It was as if he was watching to see what I did next. But I disappeared around the corner. And then had a long reflection about his admonition.

My life was not the same again after that day. Anytime I found myself engaging in any misconduct, the Priest's words would play all over again in my head and I would self-regulate and redirect my behaviour.

Yes, I felt terrible on the day he scolded me and I even thought it was unfair to scold me for playing with my friends; for only being a child.

But again, yes I am grateful that he admonished me that day! My life turned around for the better that day. His words gradually turned from thorns in my flesh to a compass and a life guide. It gave my life a whole new meaning. He certainly didn't spare the rod; and he certainly didn't spoil me. He moulded me!

Chapter
6

Primary School Escapades

Somehow, I survived my preschool ordeals. Yes, that's what I'll call it; I didn't enjoy it one bit! But I pressed on. With every incident, I grew a thick skin and learnt how to cope and move on.

So I made it into the elementary school years! I'd become a teenager by now.

One of the escapades I would like to share with you is about my first crush. Hahaha...you heard me right! I had a crush on a boy when I was 14 years old. His name was Donald and the feeling I had whenever I saw or thought about him justified what they called it – a crush! It felt like the boy's charm was crushing me and taking my breath away.

We met in church, in a Youth Group we were both members of. My heart pounded every time I saw him, no matter how many times. Just the thought and prospect of seeing him when I got to church sent a thousand butterflies to my stomach! What a feeling.

As someone who had suffered hatred and hostility all her life, I held on to this new feeling. At least there was something different in my life. Finally, there was a feeling in the world that made me smile and feel good about myself.

I am sure that there must have been times when I stared at Donald unconsciously, admiring him secretly and smiling sheepishly. Hahaha. Did other people notice? Well, I didn't really care. What I cared about was that I was feeling different. And for me, it was like, "To blazes with what anybody thought about it."

Maybe God approved of this feeling I had for Donald and wanted to compensate me for all the ill-treatment I'd suffered over the past years, because, as it turned out, he felt the same way about me!

The Youth Group met every Friday in church to discuss future projects and learn about rightful living, as supported by the bible. The Youth Group president always emphasised how important it was for us, as children of God and young people, to keep our minds and thoughts pure, for the Master's use.

Sure, my mind and thoughts were pure. But part of this mind of mine at this stage was ablaze with desire for this boy-crush of mine! Sorry, it was just what it was! Hahaha.

This fateful day, after our meeting and the Youth Group members were dispersing, I mustered courage and walked up to my crush. I had been planning this for weeks on end! You don't want to know how many times I'd started walking up to him, but my courage failed me! And I ran! Oh, I had been trying forever to tell him how I felt about him.

So I finally *made* it to him!

"Hello." I greeted him, smiling from ear to ear.
"Oh, hi." He responded excitedly too, "How are you?"
"I'm good, thanks."
"Excellent. Are you on your way home now?"
"Yes. You?"
"Sure. Should we walk together?"
"I'd like that." I answered, feeling very important. So we walked out of the church premises. Then I paused in my stride and faced him. Of course, he had to halt as well.
"Is everything alright?" He asked concernedly.

"Umm…yes…everything is fine. I…I…I want to tell you something." Was I stammering? Did I just stutter? Oh dear! Eve!

"Oh, okay then." He responded, all ears, "What is it?" He asked, smiling. This was very encouraging and a perfect cue for me. So I seized the opportunity, before my courage failed me again! Hahaha.

"I like you." There, I said it!

"I like you too."

Ummm…that was easy though. That came out too fast, didn't it? Was it a good thing or not? Did he understand me? Did he get what I meant? Maybe not. So I tried another line.

"I mean I love you." I said again, fiddling with my fingers. I couldn't look him in the face now.

"I love you too!" Alright, so he knew and understood exactly what I meant. And he felt the same way!

"Really?"

"Sure, I love you!" He reassured.

"I'm happy you do!" I said excitedly. And before I thought of anything else to say, he leaned forward and hugged me. Ah! The best feeling ever! For once, I felt like I really mattered. So I returned the hug and maybe lingered a bit too long? Because I then felt him gently pulling away.

"See you next time." He offered with a smile and started walking away.

"See you." I said, still smiling and still relishing the heavenly feeling.

Wow! Could this be true? That he liked me back? In fact, loved me? It really felt so good, especially after suffering constant cruel barrages of hatred and racism. Could this be a start of something new and magical?

****

More Than Just A Skin - Memoirs of Eve

I got my answer the very next day. No, it was no start to any fantasy feeling I was building up in my head. It was only a mirage.

The following day, I saw my crush with another girl. He had moved on from me and on to another girl. So much for being in love!

So, this was my first heartbreak! My poor 14-year old heart! Would it be strong enough to love again?

****

Well, what do you know! Two years later, this romantic heart of mine got captured again! This time around, to a boy I met when I was as young as 6 years old! That's right, the same time I started my preschool. He was there but I probably hardly noticed him. Maybe because he was tiny, hahaha.

His name was Curtis and he was my aunt's neighbour and maybe I paid no attention to him because he was always there and simply what he was – a neighbour. Maybe I saw him as nothing more than that. Or maybe because we only saw when I came for holidays in my aunt's house.

I did notice one thing though - while I wallowed in the misery and hostility I got from others, this young boy would fight for me. He always defended and looked out for me.

Can you then believe that this helpless heart of mine skipped this guardian angel to go and crush on playboy Donald, hahaha!

Thankfully, when I turned 16 and after my first crush had carelessly crushed my love, my heart finally woke up and fell in love with this guardian angel of mine - Curtis.

I was in secondary school at this time.

Chapter
7

Secondary School Adventures

After my crushed love and first heartbreak, the reality of teenage years started to kick in. As far as I'm concerned, there were three stages of teenage years: the baby teenage years – which were ages 13, 14 and 15; the hardest teenage years – which were ages 16 and 17; and then the adult teenage years – which were ages 18 and 19.

Let me explain...

When you were 13 years old, they only called you a teenager because of the 'teen' that was now attached to your age. In reality, you were still a kid! Remember that this is as far as I'm concerned, hahaha.

At age 14, you started to feel a bit different; the kid behaviour and kid feeling began to wear off a bit and you gradually started to realise that growth was rapidly overtaking you. At this age, you started noticing the opposite sex, out of curiosity and adventure. The ticklish feeling you started experiencing, begged for you to explore possibilities in relationships and see what you came up with. This would explain why I thought I fell in love with Donald; he was probably both as convinced and confused as I was, hahaha!

At age 15, those ticklish feelings started to take shape and you were surer now that you were becoming a young adult. From unsuccessful love stories and heartbreaks stemming from failed crushes, you wanted to keep it low at this age. You were sorting out your feelings and deciding whether to pursue love or not. You were busy deciding how you were going to face the hardest part of your life. Which brings me to the second stage of teenage years.

The hardest teenage years! Ages 16 and 17! What a difficult period! This was when you were trying to transition into full adulthood; but some folks still thought that you were a kid; annoying situation!

The adults would tell you that you did not belong in the adult club yet; and the kids would let you know, in no uncertain terms, that you were an adult; and should leave them alone. See the dilemma?

The hardest teenage years, ages 16 and 17 were when you started putting in your best effort to establish yourself, not only as an adult, but as a complete human being who possessed their own thoughts and could take their own decisions. You were trying very hard here to establish your independence as an entity. If only they would let you!

This stage of one's teenage years was the most dangerous because it was the one stage where, if care was not taken, a teenager could derail – from so many factors ranging from peer pressure, hormonal rages, bad associations, difficult parents, demanding society; you name it! So can you imagine dealing with all this and racism at the same time? As a teenager? Now you know why I termed it the hardest teenage years!

Finally, there was the adult teenage years – ages 18 and 19. Society, at this stage, had sort of accepted you into the league of adulthood. Why else would they always use that caveat, *'18+'* anytime they wanted to indicate what age groups could watch certain movies, for example?

****

When I started secondary school, I was 16 years old.

Exactly! The hardest teenage years! Hahaha! So you can already guess what my struggles were at this stage, right? Racism was very much still a reality for me and then there was that challenge of trying to fit in as an independent adult.

There were those who hated me outrightly. But then my silver lining was always available when it was most needed. Some people – majorly my neighbours – simply admired me and thought I was cute. Can you beat that?

"You look like a dolly!" They would tell me fondly. Of course, those kind of compliments melted my heart! And I held on to those words like they were the very air I breathed. Well, maybe they were – I needed some level of kindness to keep me going. So, in addition to the love overdose my maternal family already gave me in the home front, those kind words from my admirers also boosted my self-confidence.

One thing that continued to be regular – even though they came with their own headaches – was meeting boys. Yep! It was always a headache to worry about whether they would like me or not – I mean, there was my dark skin to consider, wasn't there?

My thinking was that young boys at this stage were first smitten by a girl just for the fact that 'she' was a girl, before other things like her bodily features or skin complexion came into play. A young boy would see a young girl then, approach her and indicate interest in going out with her. But it was only after some days – or maybe even some weeks – that he actually started noticing her other girly features. Like the curves on her face, the contours of her hips, the brightness of her smile, and of course, her skin tone.

For me, it was always a case of wishing that they would see my skin first and decide whether they wanted to go ahead with me or not. So that they could save my heart the trouble of being led on and suddenly being abandoned. This was

More Than Just A Skin - Memoirs of Eve

the headache I had! Would the boys like me or not? Would they accept me or not? Such an uncertain period for me.

Despite these uncertainties, my heart would go ahead to really like a boy – most time without my consent – only to come running back to me crying because it had been rejected, hahaha.

In fairness to the boys though, I think that some of those times, it wasn't that they didn't like me or were bothered about my skin; I think it was that stigma of being seen as odd if they went ahead to date the dark skinned girl, who was totally different from the rest of them.

This must have been what happened to these two particular boys I can vividly remember, Neil and Smith.

First, Neil.

I noticed that he would look at me fondly and would look for reasons to talk to me. In school, he would run up to me immediately we finished a class and dispersed from the classroom, to ask for one thing or the other. I knew he was just looking for an excuse to talk to me because the things he asked me about were things I knew for sure that he had, hahaha.

"Excuse me, Eve," Neil would call out before catching up with me, "may I borrow your Science note?" Really? We just finished the class and everybody took note! But I would go ahead and give him and after that, we would have no choice but to keep in touch, till I got back my note. Most of the times, he would deliberately hold on to my notes, past the time he was supposed to return it. This way, I would be compelled to reach out to him to ask for it.
Well, after Neil's unique love advances, we started seeing each other and I could tell that he really liked me. We started sitting together during recess and just

talking about little nothings. We would walk out of school together, after closing times, till he headed for his house and I headed toward mine. My helpless heart started to feel at home and relaxed. Okay, maybe it was going to work out between me and Neil.

Or maybe not.

Just few days after it looked like we had become a pair, Neil started acting strangely and avoiding me.

"Sorry, Eve," he would try very hard to explain, "I have to be in a club meeting now. Can we see later?"

But after a couple of those excuses, I got the message and left him alone. Which I thought was a relief for him, because he never bothered again to reach out to me. My dark skin had finally come into play and I was almost sure that he must have fallen under pressure by his friends to leave me alone since they would not be comfortable to mingle with me as their friend's girlfriend.

Then there was Smith.

He did not even muster enough courage to approach me by himself. Rather he tried to show me his love by using another boy.

I was sitting on a bench outside the classrooms; it was recess time. Boys and girls milled around, some chatting and laughing heartily; some checking and comparing lesson notes; some making up from previous fights and some simply hugging it out.

I wasn't seeing anybody at that time so I was sitting alone, going through my notes and eating a piece of sandwich. The few female friends I had were caught up in one activity or another. I was fine though, sometimes you just wanted to sit down alone and clear your head. Today was one of those days.

Next I knew, someone was standing right in front of me and offering a strand of flower in his outstretched hand. He was smiling confidently and probably expecting me to jump at his offering.

"Excuse me?" I demanded politely.

"Take it." Was all he said, still smiling.

"What's it for?" I asked, not accepting the flower yet.

"Come on, it's a flower," he replied convincingly, "meant specially for you." He finished.

"I know it's a flower," I responded, desperately cautioning my heart not to start jubilating.

"Yeah, so take it."

"Why are you giving me a flower though?" I demanded still.

At this point, he came to sit beside me, still holding on to the flower. He could tell that I was not going to jump at it, just because he was a boy and I was a girl, hahaha.

"Well," he began explaining, "someone asked me to give this to you." He finished, indicating the flower he was holding.

"Someone?"

"Yeah, a secret admirer."

"And who is this person?"

"Smith."

I knew Smith quite alright. He was a cool guy, a bit on the quiet side but a serious students. What I didn't know was that he was secretly admiring me. I couldn't help wondering though, why he didn't bring the flower to me directly; by himself. Was he shy? Or was he running away from being seen with me?

I decided it was the latter. And I made up my mind already that it wasn't going to work out between us. If he wasn't confident enough to approach me, then I wondered how he would stand for me. For now anyway, I decide to accept his flower.

"Oh, I see," I responded collecting the flower and taking in a sniff. It did smell lovely and I couldn't help smiling. "Thank you." I finished.
"Thank him." My flower bearer encouraged, smiling and channeling his attention to a particular direction. So I followed his gaze and saw him.

Smith was sitting afar off but opposite me, quietly and satisfactorily watching the love scene playing out. I think when I smiled, he really felt good about himself. I could even see a trace of pride and conquest on his face. As far as he was concerned, he had won me over.

As far as I was concerned, he had just lost me. Maybe if he had brought the flower by himself, I would have agreed with my over-excited heart, hahaha. But yeah, as much as I really wanted to be with a guy, I needed for him to be all over me! Crazy, right? Yep, I had my standards, regardless.

Smith waved at me and I waved back, mouthing my thank you. To which he nodded proudly. His messenger stood up at this time and started walking away from me; he had done his job. Mission accomplished!

"Bye, Eve."
"Bye." I returned, smelling the flower again and placing it right beside me. Then I went back to my sandwich and lesson note.

That was all there was to Smith and me. He never pursued further and I never bothered either. If he thought I was going to do the chasing after his flower offering, then he had another think coming. This dark-skinned girl was not a knock about, you know.

****

Secondary school passed by.

I continued to meet boys, some of which I did date for short periods and some of which I never got round to dating.

Just like in primary school years, I didn't have trouble blending in at the secondary school level. The only school period I real hated was my preschool.

I did make quite a number of friends in secondary school and I mean real female friends, whom I will tell you about shortly.

Just know for now, that I managed to survive my hardest teenage years. Somehow too, my love and relationships escapades with boys rolled by.

Chapter
8

My First Love

Curtis was a White guy and I knew he was special because of how he made me feel so loved, protected and wanted.

Like I said earlier, he had always been there, right before my nose, but I just didn't really notice him even though he was always on the lookout for me, would stand by me and fight for me, where necessary.

He was my aunt's neighbour so we always saw each other whenever I went on holidays to my aunt's house. I felt he genuinely liked me because he had enough time to observe and learn about me over the years; so if after all that time, he still showed interest in me, then he was serious about me.

We started going out officially when I was 16 years; this was in secondary school. After dealing with all those boys who were either unsure of their feelings for me or more concerned about what others thought of them dating me, I finally got it right with Curtis. He was very serious about me and was not afraid to go exclusive with me, to the visual pleasure of all who cared to know.

Curtis already knew a considerable bit about me – my background, my family, my nature and so on. So we spent the first couple of years learning about each other as far as relationships were concerned. I was starting to see him as my boyfriend and not a neighbour anymore. I was beginning to learn more about him; he treated me so gently and protected me as far as his manly strength would allow him.

****

While I was going out with Curtis, I met this guy, Larry. We had known each other right from childhood days and he used to send me flowers – as we grew up. I remember that when I was 18 years old, he proclaimed his love for me.

Sadly, he passed away before we even gave a thought to the possibility of becoming more than friends. But I must say that he was really a lovely and nice person. God bless his soul!

****

By the third year of my relationship with Curtis, we were still waxing very strong and it pleased me greatly that Curtis had stuck around, against all odds. Of course by now, both of our families were very much aware of what was going on between Curtis and me and apparently, we had their blessings.

We were loving each other with every passing day. Months developed from days and the years sped by, because before we closed our eyes and opened them, five years had gone by! Curtis and I had dated for 5 solid years! Amazing!

Then something sweet happened!

It was the weekend and we had gone out to our regular diner, The Foodies, where we hung out often. We liked to go upstairs to the open space so we could enjoy nature and not be constrained by any walls.

The evening was cool, gentle and quietly sweet. Other couples were sitting around too and enjoying each other's companies.

A waiter had come and served us so we were enjoying our order and chatting away. Curtis was telling me about this particular cousin of his who had just gotten married to his secondary school sweetheart.

"Awww...that's so sweet!" I exclaimed in sheer excitement. I loved to hear about successful love stories; remember I told you I am a helpless romantic.
"Yeah, very sweet. I'm so happy for them." Curtis responded happily too.
"True love does exist!" I declared, more to myself than to Curtis.
"Absolutely!"
"So where are they now?"
"You mean, where are they having their honeymoon?" Curtis teased me. He knew that was where I was going to. It was amazing how much he knew me; he could not only read my thoughts but could actually complete my sentences for me.

His comment made me laugh heartily. I was content with Curtis. He made me feel complete and totally loved. Five years with him and I always still had the same sweet sensations as if we had just met.

"Of course!" I teased back, "You know exactly what I mean!"
"Well, they're off to the Bahamas."
"How romantic!"
"Romantic, right?"
"Sure!"
"I know you are a romantic too." He teased again. This got me blushing and made me to look down, during which Curtis did his magic. On looking back up, I noticed that he was kneeling on one knee beside me and smiling up at me.

Now come on, I knew what that position meant! I just couldn't believe my eyes! Curtis was proposing to me!

"I don't have any ring to seal this Eve," he started saying, placing his hands on my shaky ones. I was both excited and nervous at the same time. "But will you marry me?" He finished.

"Yessss!!!" I exclaimed, standing up to accept his loving embrace. He had gotten up as I exclaimed my consent.

Sure we got the attention of the other diners, some of who clapped in agreement as they smiled at our romantic scene.

And so Curtis and I got married after five years of dating and no, I didn't care about whatever any hater thought, did or said. Yes, this dark-skinned girl found love and ended up in marriage! At the age of 21! That silver lining again!

I had finished school and was working. It seemed adulthood had somehow diluted the hostility and racism I suffered for so many years. But if you thought I had escaped life misfortunes, then you're in for some shockers! They were just getting started, the adversities.

But before I delve into them, let me finish my first love story, hahaha.

With marriage came responsibilities and of course we had to make money to feed. After all, we were our own family now.

I was working in a big firm, some sort of supplies store and I was a sales person. Curtis, on the other hand was a part-time driver. He was actually looking for a job.

One of the things I'm blessed with is my ability to blend in with people. You could say that I had a very likeable character which always endeared me to people, especially in the workplace. So in this supplies store where I worked, I had a great rapport with everybody. Without meaning to take advantage of my thriving relationship with my boss, I approached him one day to have a crucial discussion.

"Sir, may I talk to you about something?"
"Sure, Eve. What would that be?"
"Thank you, sir."

My boss was a thin 54-year old, good-natured man. I don't know about others, but he was always kind to me and often encouraged me with empowering words. *Eve, you have it in you, keep trying*, he would tell me. *Don't let anybody bring down your energy, Eve, it's all you've got*, he would point out to me. *You're a strong woman, you know that, right?* He would cheer me on. Mr. Lance was a good man.

"Sure, Eve, go ahead."
"I wanted to find out if it was possible to get Curtis anything to do around here, sir." I asked politely, silently praying that I got a favourable response. Of course, everyone in my workplace knew about me and Curtis and how much we loved each other.

Mr. Lance gave my request a brief thought and then replied, "Let's see what we can do, Eve." And on seeing me starting to show my excitement, he added without any expression on his face, "I'm not promising anything though."
"Sure, sir." I responded, knowing very well that he had become expressionless so that he didn't raise my hopes. But I knew that he was going to do whatever he could, that was the kind of person he was.
"Okay, then. I'll talk to you later."
"Thank you sir."

And work continued as usual. Till about three weeks later when he called me into his office on a Thursday afternoon. He had gone out on break and stopped by my counter on his way back.

"See me in my office when you can, will you?"

"Sure sir." I replied, trying to hide my rising excitement, I was attending to a customer and didn't want to seem unprofessional. After Mr. Lance went into his office, I attended to about ten other customers before I had a breather. This was my window of opportunity to go see Mr. Lance to hear what message he had for me. I prayed it was a good one.

I knocked and entered into his office, after he bellowed for me to come in. Then I sat down on the chair opposite him, upon him motioning for me to sit.
"Thank you sir."
"So, you don't mind if your husband worked in the same place with you?"
"Um..no...no sir," I stuttered. Again, excitement was welling up inside me; that question could only mean that something positive was going to come out of this discussion.
"I see" He replied calmly. Again, he was trying not to give any emotion away. That was typical of him though; while he was not a hostile person, he was also not outgoing. He was known to be more on the reserved side, offering support to his employees where he needed to. "What is he doing at the moment?"
"He is a driver sir, something he is only doing for the meantime. Which is why we are..."
"Will he like to work in the magazine section?" He cut me short, but not rudely.
"Of course, sir. Curtis would gladly work anywhere there is a vacancy." I replied.
"Good, so let's have him start work in the magazine section then."
"O...okay...okay sir..." I stuttered again. This was excitement being suppressed by the need to remain calm in front of him and appear professional. Mr. Lance wasn't very good with emotional outbursts.
"Can he start tomorrow?"
My, oh my! This was just too good to be true! Or was I dreaming? Did Mr. Lance just give my husband a job? Oh, my world!
"Absolutely, sir! Thank you so much! I really appreciate this! It means a lot to us, sir. We are certainly..."
"You can go now, Eve." Mr. Lance announced with a smile. I had started babbling

and showing too much emotion, which he didn't like to be entangled in, hahaha. He had to save himself the situation.

So I stood and left, not having to utter any more gratitude words because Mr. Lance had gone back to working on some papers on his desk. That was his own way of dismissing me politely.

Later that day, when Curtis picked me up after close of business, he could see that I was beaming with joy. It had been all I could do to maintain calmness while I attended to customers, after I left Mr. Lance's office.

"Someone is glowing, huh?" Curtis remarked as I joined him in the car.
"You think?" I responded, smiling from ear to ear. That was me not admitting but inviting him to guess what I was glowing about.
"Let's see," Curtis said, making a thinking face, "you've been promoted?"
"Better than that!" Was my excited response.
"Okay, I'm not sure what could be better than you getting a promotion at work..." Curtis pondered aloud.
"You have a job!" I exclaimed.
"I have a job?" he repeated, trying to make sense of what I had just said, "Of course I have a job, I'm a driver and..."
"Okay, you have another job!"
"Eve?" He called out, glancing at me briefly before returning his attention to the road. "Honey, you are not making sense, you know? Do you mind telling...?"
"I got you a job in my office!" I rattled out, clapping excitedly and mock dancing.
"You did?" Curtis asked in surprise.
"Yes, I did!"
"How, honey?"
"I talked to Mr. Lance."
"Your boss?"
"Yes! And he said you could start tomorrow! You will be working in the magazine

section!"

"Are you serious right now?" He asked, both out of shock and excitement.

"Very sure! Mr. Lance said you can start tomorrow! You have a job, honey!"

"I do!" Curtis repeated again. He was still smiling as if he couldn't believe this was happening.

The rest of our journey home, Curtis and I talked about what he was going to wear on his first day at work and how two of us were going to make sure we remained professional, being that we were going to start working in the same place.

When we got home that evening, Curtis was like a young excited child who had just been bought his favourite toy, hahaha. He was practically humming to himself while he did his evening chores and making sure that his ironed shirt was not rumpled before tomorrow, as it was hung with the rest of his clothes in the wardrobe.

And that was how Curtis started working in my office.

****

Did I mention to you earlier that I had not totally escaped life misfortunes?

Good.

Because they were not done with me yet. As a matter of fact, it looked like they were just warming up to face me head on!

****

I started noticing some strange behaviours from Curtis in our third year of marriage. For example, he had become a bit distant, especially on our way back home from work. He had stopped being his usual chatty self, talking about his day at work and asking me about mine.

He used to tease about breaking any man's head in the office, whether they be co-workers or customers, who attempted to make any passes at me. And two of us would laugh about it.

Then I would tease him too about not letting any woman steal his heart away from me. To which he would reassure me that his heart belonged to only me. And I believed him.

I still did, only that he had started giving me reasons to even as much as speculate that something was wrong. My intuition told me all was not well, but I couldn't place my hand on what exactly it was.

"You're becoming quiet these days," I initiated one day on our way home from work. I had to be sure everything was alright. At least I had to try.
"How do you mean?" He responded irritably. That was strange too.
"You don't like chatting anymore when we are going home." I pointed out, even though I knew that he understood exactly what I was talking about.
"Just tired, that's all." He replied dismissively. His tone indicated clearly that he didn't want to extend that line of discussion.
"Okay." I answered feebly, not wanting to irritate him any further. This new attitude of his was all new to me and I thought I had to tread carefully.
And so we drove home in silence that day. He refused to open up; not even when I tried to talk about other things. He just kept answering in monosyllables and even completely ignoring some of my comments.
"How is your cousin and his wife?"
"They're good."
"Any plans for a second baby yet?" They already had their first child.
"Not that I know of."

"Is everything alright at work?" I switched back to him.

"Yeah."

"Today was very hectic for me, my body aches." I tried redirecting the discussion to me.

No response.

"Mr. Lance looked very ill today, I hope he's fine." Another chance at steering the discussion to something that hopefully could get him interested.

No response still.

Alright, I wasn't trying anymore. So we drove the rest of the distance home, in silence.

****

Like I said earlier, I was in good terms with my co-workers and didn't have any issue with anybody. I hadn't even as much as argued with anybody since I started working in my office.

Most of my co-workers were married individuals so everybody minded their own business. However, there was this single lady, 22-year-old Heather, who had joined our firm recently — a couple of months ago actually. She was a vibrant, cheerful, outgoing White lady, at least this was how she came across when you first met her.

With time, you would start noticing that she was actually kind of sneaky and annoyingly mysterious. She was all up in everyone's face, making it a point of duty to be noticed. Without stating it clearly, Heather always tried to make others look incompetent, pointing out to them what they had done wrong or not done at all, and in the most condescending manner.

She worked in the same unit as Curtis — the magazine department.

I remember one time she had a fight with one of my coworkers, Mrs. Stan who worked with me in sales. Heather had walked up to two of us where we were reconciling our sales figures for that day. When she got to us, she stood over the counter and regarded us for some time as if she was the boss; she had this smirk on her face.

Both of us looked up to hear what she had to say but she just kept staring down at Mrs. Stan as if looking through her soul. Then she started tapping her fingers on the counter as if that was supposed to remind us that she was there. Well, her stupid mind-controlling game didn't work because Mrs. Stan and I ignored her and continued doing our work.

"You know this is quite disappointing?" Heather finally said. We were not sure exactly whom she was talking to so we continued to ignore her. She was still tapping on the counter.

"I found this lying on the floor yesterday...," she continued, seeing that we were consciously ignoring her. But at this point, Mrs. Stan and I looked up to see that she had placed a receipt on the counter and pointing at it with her index finger, "...in the magazine department!" she finished sarcastically.

It was a sales receipt that belonged to one of our clients who had forgotten to pick it up on his way out yesterday. But I remember that Mrs. Stan had left it on our desk so that she would remember to sort out how to deliver it to the customer. How on earth did that get to the magazine department?

"Where did you get that?" Mrs. Stan asked confusedly, reaching out to grab the receipt. But sneaky Heather slid it out of her reach. The nerve!
"I found it where you carelessly dropped it." Heather replied in the most annoying way. I looked at Mrs. Stan and could see her starting to shake visibly; I knew she was seething with rage but trying to comport herself.

"That," Mrs. Stan started saying between clenched teeth, "was on my desk yesterday, how the hell did you get hold of it?" She finished, raising her pitch a notch higher.

"Well, who knows what you came to do in my department yesterday and who you came to see…" Heather taunted and started walking away. She had left the receipt on the counter, with that trail of suspicious statement which erroneously indicated that Mrs. Stan was having an affair.

"I can't wait to punch that girl in the face!" Mrs. Stan threatened angrily.

"She must have snuck in here to pick up that receipt!" I managed to say now. I'd been speechless and just watching the drama. What was that Heather girl up to, anyway?

A couple of times, Heather had approached me to observe how Curtis was a hardworking colleague and how she enjoyed working with him. Even though she would say this with a smirk on her face, I would politely thank her for the compliment, despite the eerie feeling I always had when she was around me.

"And how about you? Are you seeing anybody? Do you have a boyfriend?" I would ask, more for the courtesy of making a conversation than out of interest. I really didn't care about what was going on in her life.

"Sure I do!" She would reply proudly. "You don't think a damsel like me would be single, do you?" She always had that smirk and sarcasm. Strange, annoying woman.

"Good for you." I would say dismissively. But she would continue.

"He is such a sweet boy, you know."

"Oh, nice."

"He pampers me and literally worships the ground I walk on."

"He must be really sweet."

And just as strangely as she had brought up the unnecessary details, she would walk away.

As annoying and irritating as talking to Heather was, I did. And that went to show that I was in talking terms with my co-workers. We were all good.

Till Curtis started acting strange and raising my suspicion. Which was confirmed when I started picking up strands of gossips here and there in the office about him. At first, it was being hushed, out of my direct hearing, that he was having an affair with somebody in the office. I heard and consciously willed myself to disregard it as what it was — a gossip.

But you know what they said about gossips, rumours and lies — there was always an element of truth in them, no matter how tiny.

Then the hushed rumours became more audible. Curtis was surely having an affair; and it was with someone in the office. This was quite confusing for me as all the ladies in our office were married; he couldn't be involved with a married woman? The few singles were men — so not even a possibility!

The only single lady in the office was Heather. But she had a boyfriend and had made it clear she was happy with him. She couldn't be cheating on her boyfriend, let alone with a married man! So who was Curtis having an affair with? This uncertainty tugged at me.

A part of me said, Confront Curtis. You two should talk about it and get it sorted. It could have been a misunderstanding and all he might need to do was explain and reassure me. Go ahead, talk to him; it's not a confrontation, it's just an innocent clarifying chat.

But the other part of me said, Trust your husband. Do you really think he would cheat on you? With someone in the same office? Right under your nose? Come on now, he deserves more credit than that, Eve, he's your husband. And have you forgotten so soon how he has always got your back? Trusting him is the best way you can reciprocate his love for you.

In the end, I chose to go with trusting Curtis. My undoing!
Maybe if I had gone ahead to confront him, it would have served as a check and maybe he would have withdrawn from the illicit affair. Maybe a confrontation would have jolted him back to reality in case he was lusting and infatuating. Maybe confronting him would have reminded him that we were not just a couple, but a married one at that. But I didn't. And he continued cheating on me, right under my nose. Not that he admitted this, though.

My world was crashing down before my eyes! This was all strange to me and I had no clue how to handle it! Who was I to blame here? The mystery woman in the office or Curtis? Or maybe myself? Maybe if I hadn't got the job for my husband in my own place of work, this wouldn't have happened. Was it my fault? Did I cause this? Did I bring this upon myself?

One day, Heather saw me crying in the ladies' room. Finding out that Curtis was cheating on me had turned me into an emotional wreck and I was just helpless. Sometimes, when I couldn't handle it anymore, I would go hide somewhere and cry.

"It is okay, Eve. Everything would be alright." Heather consoled me, coming to place her arms around me and offering me the tissue box.
"Thank you." I replied, feeling both good and uneasy at the same time. Good because it just felt a relief to have someone console me; and uneasy because Heather was not known to be a nice person, nobody liked her in the office. So why was she being nice to me?
"You'll be fine, okay?"
I nodded and thanked her again. Then continued dealing with the new reality of Curtis' betrayal.

****

I think the worst part of finding out – more like confirming – the affair was whom it was with. ***Curtis had been having an affair with Heather!***

Heather! The same person who told me she was already in a relationship? Heather! The same person who consoled me when I was crying my heart out? Cheating with my husband? In the same office? Right in front of me? So she was being nice before me but sneering and laughing behind my back. Unbelievable!

Curtis! My husband! Cheating on me? With my co-worker? In the same office? In the job I got him? This was how he was repaying me for loving him as a wife and caring about his welfare? This was why he had been giving me attitude lately? He was trying to deflect my attention!

For some time, I blamed myself and suffered severe guilt. I convinced myself that I was responsible for what had happened. I had exposed Curtis to this temptation. I had pushed him into the arms of another woman. I beat myself up and wallowed in regret for months, torturing and taunting myself.

I yearned for Curtis to at least admit what he had done to me. I just needed some sort of closure; so I would even play out his apology line in my head. "Sorry it happened."

But as much as I wanted him to own up and apologise, I was too shocked, too dazed and too drained to talk about or pursue it. I was busy blaming myself, which I probably inadvertently projected on Curtis because even though he never admitted his illicit affair with Heather, he picked up on my self-pity energy fast and started acting as if I was to blame for what had happened.

But what did that matter anyway. The damage had been done! The trust had been broken! The bond had been severed! Everything had changed. Things were not the same anymore. And while I hoped they would soon normalize, a part of me told me that was not going to be the case. I feared maybe the worst was still to come.

The next six months was a rough patch in my marriage with Curtis. Of course he continued seeing Heather and in all honesty, I wasn't quite sure whether I should fight them or hope that things would normalize once again. For the greater part of the time after finding out about his illicit affair with Heather, I was simply in shock mode and at a loss as to what to do.

Again I had chosen the gentle way – hope that things returned to normal. And once more, it backfired on me. Not only did Curtis and Heather continue their illicit affair, but half a year later, the unthinkable happened. Wanna guess?

****

I woke up one day to realise that half of Curtis' belongings were missing. Where were they? More importantly, where had he gone to? As strange and stupid as it sounded to me, I told myself that maybe he needed some space and had gone to clear his head somewhere. I was feeling very sad that my marriage was shaking in its foundations. What could I do? I had no inkling where Curtis had gone to; I only hoped that he would be back soon.

I was wrong.

Curtis was going to be away for a long time! No, he wasn't dead; and no, he had not gone to clear his head somewhere. In fact, his head was crystal clear and he knew exactly what he was doing. But nothing prepared me for it.

It was after a few days that we all put two and two together in the office -

Heather had also been absent for a couple of days and I think while there was that unspoken understanding of what had happened, my coworkers refused to confront me with it. But it was obvious, wasn't it? The handwriting was clearly written on the wall.

Curtis and Heather had eloped!

Gone! Vanished! Disappeared! They both decided to leave together, damning what anybody thought about them or the effect their action had on the people they left behind. Curtis left me behind to suffer the shame. Curtis left his wife, to run off with a young lady he met in the office where his wife had got him a job! What an irony! And how shameful to me; it was highly humiliating.
The shame was too much for me; I always felt that I could just become invisible so that my coworkers would stop looking at me that way. Some pitied me, I think some blamed me, but generally, they all looked at me with that expression of, 'What a shame, how will she cope now?"

But more than the shame was the pain. Deep, excruciating pain! I had been hurt to the core of my being. It felt like the end of the world for me! Where exactly was I supposed to start from? How exactly was I supposed to face people? Oh my world!
My marriage had lasted only three and a half years!

More painfully was the fact that Curtis was my first. It hurt deeply because he was my first in so many things. He was the first to date me officially; he was the first to become intimate with me; he was the first to marry me; he was the first to call me wife. The list was endless! It hurt so badly!

****

"I'm too trusting!" I cried uncontrollably. "I trusted Curtis too much!"

Staying at home all alone, after Curtis absconded, was too much for me. Our house reminded me of so much about him. Everywhere held a memory of him and the fond times we shared together.

So I had gone to my grandmother's to stay for some time – grandpa had passed away by this time. But I needed to be around people I could really trust and who didn't take that for granted.

My grandmother was as devastated – if not more – as I was. She cried with me, hugged me, comforted me, soothed me, encouraged me, inspired me with her words and more importantly, loved me.

"It's not a crime to have trusted your husband, my child." She soothed me, not condemning me as I was doing to myself.
"But look where it got me!" I lamented.
"It's not your fault dear child."
"Curtis took me for granted. I'm too naïve!"
"You are an angel, Eve dear. Naivety is not an invitation to be treated poorly by others."
"Was it wrong to be loyal to my husband? Where exactly did I go wrong?"
"You did nothing wrong, my dear. This has got nothing to do with you but everything to do with Curtis."
"I'm finished! Where do I start from?"
"You are certainly not finished my dear child!" Grandmother's tone had gone a pitch higher and I knew that she was scolding me subtly and at the same time trying to console me. "You are certainly not going to allow one person to control your life and happiness..."
"But that one person is my husband, gran!" I countered bitterly.
"Husband or not, no one has any right to determine how your life turns out, unless you let them."
"Gran! Gran! Gran!" I wailed and fell into her arms, where she held me closely,

tightly and with all the warmth and love in the world.

"It's okay my angel. You know that Curtis made a choice of leaving an angel to run away with the devil." She consoled me.

"It hurts grandma!"

"Of course, my child. It would hurt now but it's his loss!"

At the moment, I couldn't see past my pain how what had just happened was a loss for Curtis. He was the one who had run away with another woman – they were probably happy together, wherever they were. On the other hand, I was the one hurting. How was this his loss?

"How, grandma? How is this Curtis' loss?" I voiced out my confusion.

"You'll see, my child. You'll see." She promised me.

And yes! My mother did reach out to comfort me! She was so sad for me and even sadder that she hadn't been there for me as much as she would have loved to.

Somehow, my aunts also reached out and comforted me in the best way they could. My family was the best! Did I mention that before? Hahaha.

However, despite all the love they showered on me and how desperately they tried to help me cope with the situation, the hurt only seemed to escalate and started affecting me emotionally, health-wise and psychologically. I'm sure they feared that something terrible was going to happen to me.

Luckily, I pulled through. Time really did heal wounds – not saying that I really did heal; I think I only got around to dealing and accepting the situation.

One of the things that helped me deal with the heartbreak was quitting my job and going to work somewhere else. Sure you can relate to this? Too much memory of Curtis in the office and more unfortunately, too much stigma to bear.

****

With every second, minute, day, week and month that rolled by, I got more and more used to not having Curtis around. I started preparing myself mentally to move on.

I dare say that at some point even, I actually got angry! But not with myself. I got angry with Curtis, relieved myself of all the blames I'd carried for so long and totally poured them on him. Yes, he was at fault here; he was the one who did the wrong thing. He was the one who walked away; he was the irresponsible one, the immature one.

My self-worth was very important to me so I picked myself up, gathered what was left of it from the heartbreak – which was very little, hahaha – and moved on. My heart and I understood each other and we knew how we rolled. I trusted it to get ready to love again; to trust again and to be loyal again. Maybe not so much anymore, hahaha. Just enough to make my future relationships enjoyable and memorable.

****

Chapter
9

My Second Relationship

Thanks to my angelic charm – hahaha – I found another job soon after I left the supplies shop, my former office.

This time around, it was a gym; what better way to heal from a major heartbreak than working in a fitness outfit! Work out all the bad memories and negative energy, isn't it? Hahaha.

Grandma was right; Curtis was the one who lost out, because this pretty, confident, witty and humourous me bounced back. I wasn't sure how he was doing with Heather but I was certain that I was doing better than two of them! I had my vibe back! And I was ready to smash the world, yeah!

Working in the gym was both refreshing and exhilarating for me. It was a burst of new and fresh air; the dawn of new beginnings.

Even though I was ready to move on in life and put the past behind me, I was still nursing my heart and being a bit too protective of it. I wasn't quite sure I was ready just yet, to be involved with any guy in any relationship.

So I was just content watching clients come in to exercise. I observed and realised that people were in different categories in the journey called life. Everybody was running their own race and facing their own lane.

There were couples who came together to exercise and you would see the mutual love between them; the common goal of being fit and helping each other grow. Then there were individuals who were there because it was a condition for sustaining their relationships. Their boyfriends or girlfriends had mandated them to go get fit or kiss their relationships goodbye, hahaha.

Of course there were those who came to keep fit just because it was part of their personal goals. No obligations, no deadline, no pressures. Just being themselves and striving to be better.

I must admit though - and this is not to make those of you who are not fitness inclined feel guilty, hahaha – there was a sense of accomplishment and fulfilment that working out and being fit brought with it. Your mind was decluttered and clearer; your body felt lighter and more agile and you just knew within yourself that you were in a good place.

****

Apparently, while I was observing the clients who milled in and out of our gym centre, someone else was watching me closely. How did I know? Oh, he told me, himself.

"I've been admiring you from afar, you know." A deep male voice announced to me one day at the gym. I was packing away some exercise cones which I'd just finished using. So I looked up and started into the smiling face and searching eyes of Joe, one of my coworkers.

Joe was a tall, White guy, in his late 40s. I had always seen and related to him as a coworker and nothing more. However, he was an easy-going person and blended well with others. I know that we had a few chit chats in the past but that was all there was to it; remember I told you I wasn't ready just yet to get involved with anybody. So I willed myself not to even think in that direction when I saw guys.

But this Joe guy had obviously been looking at me differently; maybe more than just a coworker.

"You have?" I responded jokingly.
"Hello, Eve." He greeted now.
"Hi, Joe."
"Yes, I have been admiring you."
"And...?"
"And I like how you carry yourself. Plus you're a beautiful woman."
If he thought I was going to blush or fall head over heels in love with him immediately, he had a long think coming! I was done being smitten and I had warned my heart to behave too. I believed it was cooperating. Hahaha.
"Thank you." I responded, carrying the cones and walking towards the store.
"Would you like to have lunch with me?" He called out after me.
"Nope!" I bellowed back, coming out of the store and walking away.

I could picture him smiling at my behaviour and muttering to himself, "Women." Something told me he was going to try his luck again, men didn't just give up like that. They loved chasing because then they felt a sense of accomplishment when women finally said yes. Men were typical hunters, hahaha.

And so did Joe hunt me tirelessly, for the next couple of months, till I finally agreed to go out with him. And this was officially my second relationship; the very next time I would open up my heart after my husband eloped with another woman. However, I couldn't really say I was one hundred percent smitten, I was still guarding my delicate heart here. Did you blame me? Hahaha.

Joe and I started dating and everything was going on fairly well. Yup, there was a little 'but;' Joe drank too much alcohol and smoked excessively. Not that was against drinking and smoking but come on, it was just too much. And for someone who worked in a gym and was supposed to be health-conscious?

Our relationship progressed regardless.

And exactly when I was 31 years of age – Joe was 47 years old at this time – I moved to the English-speaking part of Europe. My mother wasn't from the Anglophone region so I had grown up, not speaking English, even though there were a lot of White people in my environment.
Actually, Joe and I moved together.

On arrival, we started the whole dragging process of settling in and getting accustomed to a new environment – getting a house, meeting new neighbours, making new friends, forming and starting new routines, getting used to new places, new way of life, new culture, new belief systems, new societal expectations, new food, you name it. The process just seemed to go on forever.

Anyway, we lived through the process and stabilized gradually.

After a while, I got a job in another gym outfit. Looked like I was stuck in the health sector, yeah? Hahaha.

My life went on, and so did my relationship with Joe, who was very helpful with the process of settling in. Sadly, he continued drinking and smoking. And as much as I didn't believe in changing people, (you couldn't really change anybody, could you?) I had to have a discussion with him about the effect his bad habits was having on his health.

"You know you have to tone it down with this drinking and smoking, Joe." I initiated one day. We were dining out and I couldn't help notice how he kept downing bottles upon bottles of alcohol.

"I'm good." He responded, continuing to gulp down the alcoholic content.

"No, you're not, Joe." I disagreed immediately, almost irritably.

"Hey, take it easy girl." He said in his usual playful manner. He never seemed to take anything seriously, especially when it had to do with things he believed were already part of him.

"Funny you should say that to me, Joe," I couldn't help being sarcastic, "because you are the one who needs to take it easy with drinking and smoking."

"Don't start now, honey," He started saying a bit seriously, "you knew I drank and smoked before we started dating, didn't you? So, what now?"

"I'm not saying you should quit dear. Just saying be careful. Maybe you shouldn't drink and smoke as much." I advised, but I already knew that he wasn't going to take any of it.

"I'm good, okay?" He assured me again.

"I hope so." I responded feebly.

But Joe's drinking and smoking habits persisted. And somehow, I got used to living with it. After all, he was never abusive; nor did it affect his behaviour. He was always as helpful as ever. So I had to accept the situation and move on; it wasn't everything that one could control, you know.

Sometimes, we had to deal with our circle of influence – those things we could control and had power over; and then starve our circle of concern – the stuff we had absolute zero control over. Changing someone was really close to impossible.

Trying to get Joe to smoke or drink less – at the age of 47 – was absolutely in my circle of concern. It was certainly something I couldn't change, even if I dedicated the whole 24 hours of the day trying! Joe was an adult and had lived with this habit practically all his life! What I had to do was either live with it...or leave.

Why didn't I leave, come to think of it? Maybe it didn't really bother me that much. Or maybe I just didn't want to be alone again, just yet. As a helpless romantic, it was difficult for me not to be with a guy; not for long periods of time. Surely a lady needed to be with a man. Hey, don't go raising your eyebrows at me, okay? This wasn't my law, you know. God Himself designed it that way. So don't go blaming me for needing a man's company. Hahaha.

****

"Oh, wow! Look what I found!" I exclaimed to myself on this fateful day. I was sorting some of my documents and books when this envelop fell out from a stack of papers.

It was an envelope that my father had given me years ago, before we parted and he went back to Africa. Being that it had been a long time, the envelope had become quite old and faded; but one thing still stood out – his address on it!

I did know that my father was a retired doctor but what I didn't know was where he was living at the moment. Now, finding the envelope started stirring in me the longing to see him again. But where on earth did I start looking for him?

After a few days, I was convinced I wanted to see my father again. No matter how long it had been that he was absent in my life, there was always that natural attraction to him because he was my father after all. You couldn't cheat nature, could you?

So off I went to the Library Directory, where I started digging. And there! I found my father's old address! But the real excitement was that listed under this old address, was his new one! My father was living in the same region as I was! What an interesting turn of events!

Now the issue was how to go about meeting him. He hadn't seen me in years so I wasn't even sure that he would be interested in seeing me? I had a strong feeling he would, of course. But how did I make the move? I had no idea how to address him or what exactly to say when he picked my call. And then there was the reality that I did not speak English – yet.

So, Joe to the rescue! He was the best person to make this happen! He could help me talk to my father on my behalf.

And he did!

"Hello there, am I speaking to Mr. Kofi please?" Joe finally put a call across to my father. Once he dialed the number, he put it on speaker so that I could follow along.

"Yes, you are. Who am I speaking with please?" My father responded gently and politely. He still exuded that calm, soft-natured personality that he was. His voice had become a bit deeper with aging, but it was the same voice I heard last, so many years ago.

"My name is Joe and I'm a friend of Eve's." Joe explained and you could practically feel my dad's reaction at the mention of my name. He was silent for a couple of seconds, apparently trying to assimilate and figure out if the name he had just heard was the same one he had given to the child he birthed years ago. Hahaha.

"Eve? My Eve?" He asked now, half-confused and half-expectant. I could sense all of this by the tone of his voice, his unseen non-verbal communication, Joe's reactions and facial expressions.

"Yes, Mr. Kofi, I mean Eve, your daughter." Joe confirmed.

"Eve!" My dad exclaimed excitedly. "Where is she now?"

"She's right here."

"She is? She is! May I speak with her? Does she want to speak with me?" My father rattled out uncontrollably. His excitement was contagious because found myself smiling excitedly too.

Joe had to, once in a while, cover the mouthpiece so he could tell me or explain something my father had said or asked.
"She would very much like to speak with you but her English is very minimal." Joe pointed out innocently; both men laughed and I smiled in mock embarrassment as Joe let me in on my dad's question and the response he had given him.
"Of course! That's understandable! Let me hear her voice anyway." My father insisted. So Joe handed me the phone.
"Hello!" I said in my thick accent. I was both shy and excited.
"Hello Eve! It's good to hear from you after a long time!" He said and of course Joe quickly interpreted this to me.

And that was how I reconnected with my father; we kept talking to each other with the help of Joe and as time went by, we then set up a proper and formal meeting.

****

Last time I saw my dad, I was only 3 years old. So you could imagine how nervous I was to meet him physically after more than 3 decades! Both of us had lived in very different cultures, with different family members and only clinging to the little knowledge we had of each other before parting.

While his own memories would have been more tangible as an adult that he already was, mine was as faint as my 3-year old brain could store. It had been a pretty long time!

Still with the help of Joe, my father and I finally met and it was the strangest, most awkward, but interesting meeting of the century! Hahaha.

He didn't know whether to hug me or not; I didn't know how to greet him. But we both knew that we were pleased to see each other. Joe did his best to dissipate the slight tension and awkwardness between my father and me, thanks to him!

Anyway, I met my father after so many years and reestablished a link. With time, he introduced me to his family, my Black family. And I did meet my half-brother! Exciting!

One thing I would tell you upfront was that they were so pleasant and warm; very welcoming. I had always heard about how hospitable the Africans were but of course, I hadn't experienced it. So here I was, feeling it first-hand.

They were all over me, trying to make me as comfortable as they could; making conscious effort to feed me to my stomach's brim – told you the African people believed in body evidence. You had to show how healthy you were by showing off your robust body; hey, I didn't say fat. Hahaha.

As a matter of fact, when my African family met me for the first time, they all thought I was sick! How could I be so thin! And there I was with my model body, thinking that I was healthy and fit, hahaha.

Tell you the truth? I totally enjoyed the attention, care and concern they showed me. I loved the experience; it made me feel so special. They made me feel so special. My father was obviously trying to make up for all the lost years! It was a good compensation though, especially whenever it drove Joe to jealousy, hahaha.

Yes, Joe started feeling I was getting too much attention, seeing the way my father's family pampered me; and worse still, when other Blacks admired me openly. They all thought I was cute and adorable. I was, wasn't I? Hahaha.

****

Then the misfortunes came knocking again. Told you they weren't done with me yet. It was as if anytime I was about to be happy, they gathered — the misfortunes, I mean — and devised their next attack on me. Once my relationship with Joe and my African family started to stabilize, a can of unfortunate events was let open.

"I feel dizzy." Joe had started complaining lately. To which I encouraged him to rest more and avoid very strenuous activities. In reality, he wasn't really doing such routines, but at least I had to say something.

I suspected it could be linked to his excessive drinking and smoking habits but I wasn't ready to start another argument with him. He said he was okay and I left it at that.

But the situation persisted and with time, it changed to chest pain. He would complain about severe chest pain and would be in agony for a few minutes, during which I would run around helplessly, trying to do something to alleviate his pain.

He had blatantly refused to visit the hospital, as I'd suggested. He just kept saying he was fine. But he just kept getting worse.

One evening, I had come back from work and Joe and I were just relaxing. I was watching the television; he was half-watching and half-checking his phone. As usual, he had a bottle of alcohol beside him and a stick of cigarette in between his left index and middle fingers. He hardly did anything without accompanying it with any of those.

Suddenly, he dropped the cigarette and started twitching, clutching his chest. I quickly grabbed the cigarette stub and threw it into the tray beside him, to avoid a fire outbreak. Then I faced him.

"What, Joe!" I enquired worriedly. He was letting out a painful shriek, crying like a baby.
"My chest! I can't breathe!" he managed to say in between bouts of cry.
"Let's go to the hospital right away." I said; this time around, it wasn't a suggestion and as I was saying it, he was nodding his head vigorously. Apparently, he was in dire pain and was desperately agreeing to be taken to the hospital!
"Okay, let me grab my purse..." I started saying, running into the bedroom. But I stopped in my track as Joe let out another painful scream, which had me racing back to where he was.

At this time, his breathing was very short and laboured, his heartbeat was seizing! I was as confused as hell; what was I to do? So I forgot about grabbing my purse and started making efforts to help him off the ground. "Come on, Joe, let's go."

He managed to put his arm around my shoulder but that was all he could do. The pain could not let him move and as much as I tried to exert my own energy to lift him up, I couldn't. Joe was a huge guy and without any effort from him, it was impossible for feeble me to help him up.

Then his arm fell off from behind my shoulder and his whole body went limp. He was motionless!

"Joe!" I screamed.
"Come on, Joe, let's get you to the hospital now!" I cried.
"Joe!"
"Joe, what are you doing?" I yelped, pulling his limp arm to try to lift him up.
"Joe?" I called out when I suddenly realised that he had stopped crying and

clutching his chest. "Joe?" I shook him as I also noticed that his eyes were closed. Was he sleeping?

"No! No!! No!!!" I suddenly wailed. Reality had hit me. The reality that Joe was dead!

"Joooooooe!!!" I cried. "Joe, please don't do this!"

And honestly, the rest of what happened next was like in slow motion for me. It felt like I wasn't part of that reality. I must have done everything like a zombie because I felt so detached from the present reality. I watched Joe's lifeless body on the floor for some time, then absent-mindedly made a few calls, after which the process of picking up and lodging Joe's body in a mortuary commenced.

Mechanically, I went through all the necessary steps of registering his death, getting his death certificates and preparing for his burial. I was able to contact some members of his family who made it to the burial. And just like that, Joe was gone, exactly three years after we started seeing each other.

I was alone again! A 34-year old single lady! Hit again by another life catastrophe.

****

By now, my heart had learnt to toughen up, heal and move on. My attitude was that of, *'Bring it on.'* It was like I had braced myself for whatever came my way.

But as much as my heart wanted to comply with me and not open up to meeting new guys, it couldn't help but give a few of them chances.

For example, I let myself open up to meeting more of Black men, going on some dating sites and meeting some guys, leading to brief dating but which never really worked or lasted. So we ended up just being friends. This was exactly what happened to a Ghanaian guy I met at work — we remained friends but not a couple.

Somehow, I think this was me unconsciously protecting my heart from further aches. Moreover, as a young Christian woman, I was just plain careful of whom I got involved with, in a relationship. Intimacy was not just a moral factor, it was also a form of emotional bonding and I had to protect myself spiritually.

Chapter
10

My Third Relationship

Could it get any worse than the racism I suffered, losing my husband to another woman and losing a boyfriend to the cold hands of death?

Could my suffering be more than those? Were those not the worst things that could have happened to me?

Nope! The worst were yet to come!

One of which was my leg problem. I had varicose veins. And on this particular day, I had gone to the hospital to have it checked out as I had been experiencing some discomfort.

And to add to my distress and irritation, they couldn't do anything to relieve me of my uneasiness. Instead, they asked me to come back another time.

So I was walking home upset. But then I thought to myself, why don't you go somewhere and cool off?

Good idea!

The cooling off venue was KFC. I went upstairs to eat and relax. So I placed my orders, was served and I started eating. Finally, some peace!

Or so I thought, hahaha.

A young, good-looking guy walked in after some time. To tell you the truth, I was enjoying the feeling of eating and being all by myself. But I did notice this guy's physical features because he did walk quite close to my table to sit.

There was an empty table separating his own and mine but it didn't stop him from starting a conversation.

"Hi there," he greeted politely and upon me looking up and smiling, he proceeded, "mind if I join you?"

Yes, I mind, my head said.

"No, it's fine." My mouth countered. That must have come from that gentle heart of mine which was always concerned for me and wanting me to have a male company in my life. That love-stricken heart of mine. Hahaha.

"Thank you for accepting me." He offered as he joined me on my table.
"You're welcome." I responded, having the opportunity to take in the rest of his physical traits. He was handsome, not quite on the tall side and certainly English.
"So, should I order more food for you?"
"Oh, thanks, but I'm okay with what I've ordered. I am actually full."
"That means you don't eat much, do you?"
"Well, maybe not, but that would depend on what quantity you regard as much.
"If you can't go another round of what you just ordered, then you don't eat much." He explained jokingly and smiling. I appreciated his sense of humour and how down-to-earth he was, or appeared to be.
"I am health-conscious, you know. I work in a gym so I have to..."
"Oh, not this health nonsense!" He countered, still smiling, but I could hear a tone of seriousness. Well, he sure must have his opinions.
"You don't like talking about health?

More Than Just A Skin - Memoirs of Eve

"Never mind. I was just joking." He dismissed. "So, what's your name, if I may ask?"

"Eve." I provided, then asked, "And you?"

"Adam." He replied and we both laughed at the joke. He did have a good sense of humour.

"Are we trying to re-enact the creation story?" I asked and we both laughed again.

"I'm Ken." He said finally.

"Nice to me you, Ken." I responded. Surely, I was relaxing and forgetting that I was upset earlier. Good idea to have come to KFC to cool off.

And that was how Ken and I met and started seeing each other. I did think it was such an unusual place to meet him. To think that I'd been upset and had gone there for the sole purpose of calming myself down. The last thing on my mind that day was starting a relationship with any guy. I wasn't even as much as expecting to meet anybody that day.

But remember what I told you about fate? It blew like a breeze which you didn't know where it would settle. I would have thought that I would meet a guy that I would end up dating, maybe in a cozy mall, a party, a club or something. Not in a busy fast food place. But what did I know; you could meet anybody anywhere! As far as that's what fate had already determined, isn't it?

Ken and I got very close and all, but our relationship didn't quite work out to the point of marriage, unfortunately. We both had very diverse views and opinions about life. So we couldn't get married.

Despite being a Christian, Ken believed that women were the weaker vessels; to be lorded over by men; and only needing to be submissive. Ken believed that women didn't have any say when it came to the important things in life, which included relationships.

He was sort of too domineering for my liking. I was too strong for this kind of profile he had for women. This was me who had gone through thick and thin; this was me who had been forced to stand up for myself in so many occasions. Now he wanted to suppress all that and have 'me' just be a yes-man to him? Nah! Wasn't gonna happen.

So our relationship didn't lead to marriage, it didn't last that long. Even though something did happen between us that was going to last for a very long time!

I will tell you what it was, shortly.

****

Even though it wasn't quite working the way both of us would have wanted it, Ken and I remained friends.

He was also a Christian, but not a Catholic. Nevertheless, he brought me back to Christ. Yes, back to Christ; I had backslid maybe a little too much, hahaha.

One big thing that Curtis' disappearance did to me was that it had made me to stop going to church. I had not given up on God nor did I stop believing in His existence, but I had lost that zeal to go to church. It felt like, what was the need of going to church if I'd been hit that badly? It did feel that I had been abandoned. So I had kept to myself and stayed away from church for a very long time.

But Ken made me to come back close to God.
Our relationship progressed very well and I was happy, at the very least. If not for anything, he made me feel comfortable in who I was and what I stood for. He made me to become positive again, opening my eyes to the beauty of God's supremacy and the endless possibilities that came with knowing Him.

More Than Just A Skin - Memoirs of Eve

But…

Did you remember I mentioned that a can of unfortunate events were let loose on me? Right, here was another bomb!

****

Ken and I was supposed to meet on this particular day so I was sitting down somewhere, waiting for him. Then I realised that I couldn't stand up when I wanted to get up to use the restroom. I hadn't sat down for so long so it couldn't have been that my bones were stiff!

I sat back down, mentally giving myself some time before trying to stand up again. Maybe I had stood up too quickly. I was just mulling over different possibilities.

Next time I tried to stand up again, it was the same challenge; I just couldn't get up. I couldn't stand up on my feet! What was happening? Something was definitely wrong!

I picked up my phone and instead of calling Ken, I called my father. Yes! We were still in touch.

"Are you alright, Eve?" My father asked concernedly when he picked up my call and heard the panic in my voice.
"I'm not sure, father, I can't stand up!" I said, obviously upset.
"Where are you?" He asked, quickly picking up on the urgency in my tone and deciding not to waste any more time asking me how it had happened. I couldn't help but notice, so proudly, this part of him that was all about protecting me. Yes, that could also have been the doctor in him in action, but I also knew he was just trying to save his daughter.

So I told him where I was and he sprang into action immediately.

"Okay, I'll come as soon as I can! Just remain calm."
"Okay, father. Thank you." I said, a bit relieved. Then I called an ambulance.

****

Chapter
11

Vital Updates...

Yes, I remember I'm owing you the details of what happened between Ken and me that I told you lasted for a long time.

And yes, I know I need to flesh out that part of my story that took me to the hospital. You mean, what happened to me? I hear you asking or wondering, **so what was the problem? Why couldn't you stand up that day?**

Not to worry, okay? I will certainly get back to those pieces of puzzles; but first, let me fill you in on some important updates.

Let's start with my mother.

My mother...

You remember I moved to the English-speaking part of Europe when I was 31 years old, right? Good.

Now before I moved, my mother was diagnosed of cancer. I was 30 years old at that time. According to the doctors, it was incurable and that dreaded message had been shared with her already, 'You only have about six months to live.'

I remember that day vividly; I was at work and had no inkling of the kind of horrible news I was going to receive.

"Hello, Eve dear." My mother called me that day. Since she got sick, we had become closer as we talked often on the phone. At the end of the day, nature was nature and no matter how much we tried, we couldn't cheat it. The bond between a mother and a child is so deep that not even being apart can sever it. A mother could never really neglect the child she bore! Nor could a child ever forget the one who brought him or her into this world.

"Hello, mother. Are you alright?" I asked. Of course I already knew she was not okay, she had been doing those medical checkups and receiving some treatments. The last thing she felt was okay. But there was a deeper sadness in her voice as we spoke.

"I am, my child. But there is something I have to let you know."

"What is it mother?" My heart skidded and then sped up ten times more than the usual beat.

"You have to be strong, my child..." she started saying calmly but sadly.

That expression! That was what the nurses or doctors told you when they were about to break a sad news to you.

You have to be strong! You have to stay calm! We tried all we could...

"Mother! Are you alright?" I panicked.

"The doctor says I don't have much time left." She said, still in her calm tone This was apparently hard for her to do; it was not the easiest of messages for a mother to deliver to her child. And yet, she really had to tell me.

"Time for what, mother?" I asked in denial. I already knew what she was talking about but just couldn't wrap my head around it.

"I have only 6 months to..."

"Noooo! Mother, you are not going anywhere...you will be fine...you are just..." My voice trailed off as I burst out into uncontrollable tears. And the silence from her end told me that she was sobbing too.

She kept going for her treatments and in all honesty, we all hoped that she would get better. And what do you know; she actually started getting generally better.

****

Exactly one month after I moved though, my dear mother passed away! She left this world at the very young age of 49! Very sad!

Fortunately, after I found and met my father, I told her about my mother and was able to get them to talk a few times before she died.

Till some minutes before my mother gave up the ghost, I was on the phone with her. And while this brought us way closer and bonded us more tightly, it left this unbearable pain in my heart. To think that I was talking to her as she was dying – and I couldn't do anything! Horrible, horrible feeling!

"You take care of yourself, my child..." she was telling me on her death bed, her breathing laboured.
"You'll be fine, mother..." I was still insisting and believing.
"You are blessed, Eve..." she continued weakly.
"And you too, mother..." I sobbed sadly.
"You know I love you, right?" She told, more than asked, me.
"I love you too, mother and you'll be f..."
"I have to go now, dear child..." And her voice trailed off as the line went dead.

Less than an hour later, she passed.

For me, it was the worst experience ever. She was so young! Only 49 years! The pain stayed with me for a long time and even though I mourned her, I was happy that before she died, we had become close and bonded as mother and daughter.

My grandmother...

A year after my mother was diagnosed of cancer, I moved. I was 31 years old then, remember?

And then, exactly a year after I moved, another death hit me. This time around, it was my dearest grandmother! The angel who had raised me.

My sister had come to visit me. And we had hugged and laughed and did some catching up. There was just so much to talk about! We were very close!

"And how is grandmother?" I had asked her finally. Enough of the gists and gossips. Time to ask after my kind, generous and wise grandmother.
"She's fine..." my sister answered but you could see that her mood had changed, "...she's getting by." Of course grandmother had aged and wasn't in the best of shape, health wise.
"It is well with her blessed heart." I prayed.
"Amen!" My sister agreed.

The very next day, my sister and I were sorting our clothes for laundry; it was a weekend. Then a call came in for me.

"Who is that now?" I asked in mock irritation and going to get the phone which was on top of my dressing table. We were just having so much fun, lazing around, teasing each other, pillow-fighting and laughing so hard while sorting our laundry.
"Who have you been giving sleepless nights?" My sister teased, giving me a mischievous wink. She was referring to the phone call, insinuating that it was a man.
"You think I'm a heartbreaker like you?" I teased her back and we both laughed.
I reached my phone just in time; before the call could disconnect. It had rung for

a while as my sister and I bantered each other.

"It's aunty!" I managed to announce to my sister before I answered the call.

"Hello aunty!" I greeted excitedly. "How is every…"

"There's sad news dear." She cut me off and announced sadly. It was unlike her to interrupt like that so whatever was her reason to do so, must be serious.

"Sad news?" I repeated, looking at my sister with a confused look, which she mirrored on her own face. What sad news could that be, two of us wondered silently.

"Your grandmother is gone…" My aunty managed to say before she started sobbing.

"How do you mean, gone?" I asked, already knowing full well what that meant.

At this point, my sister sprang up from the bed and grabbed the phone from me. Which gave me the opportunity to walk like a zombie to the bed, where I stared into space.

"Hello aunty!" I heard my sister greet loudly, but it sounded so faint in my ears, almost like an echo. "Aunty! What happened to grandmother?" my sister asked as she too started sobbing.

Why wasn't I sobbing? Why was I dry-eyed?

Oh, yeah, that was because I was gently slipping into insanity. I had no awareness of where I was or what I was doing. I could see fleeting movements intermittently in the room — that must have been my sister crying hysterically and throwing herself on the floor.

As for me, I was thinking, 'This must be the end of the world.' And sane people didn't exist when the world was about to come to an end. That was exactly the state I was in.

Grandmother couldn't be dead! Come on! How? No, not grandmother! Oh, dear Lord! What was happening? What have I done to deserve all this misfortunes?

"Eve! Eve! Eve!" Someone was calling my name. But again, it sounded very faint. That must have been God calling me home. Yes, God was calling me to go and see my grandmother, at least to tell her goodbye.

"Eve! What are you doing?" The faint voice said now. Then someone grabbed me and started vigorously flinging my arm. It was at this point I came back to reality and noticed that I had squeezed a glass till it broke in my hand. And I had continued squeezing! Blood was gushing out of my hands and my sister was trying to get me to let go of the shards which had cut deeply into my flesh!

Apparently, while my sister cried and rolled on the floor, I had walked into the kitchen absent-mindedly and gone straight to the sink to wash the dishes. Told you I was going insane! The first thing I got my hands on must have been a glass cup which I had unleashed the frustration of my loss and pain on.

All the tears I had not shed, I had transformed into rage and was letting it out by squeezing. Unfortunately for both me and the glass, it was the first thing I grabbed as my rage was released.

"Do you want to hurt yourself?" My sister continued yelling, both upset and afraid. Once I released the shards, she ran to get the first aid box. And while she tended to my cut, then and only then, did I start crying.

I cried so hard. I cried uncontrollably. I cried out all the pent up pain I had bottled up for years. It was that kind of cry that was about not only what had happened but also about other things in the past.

I cried, remembering all the time my grandmother shielded me from racist pangs. I cried, remembering the first day she took me to school. I remembered the dresses she crocheted for me; the dolly she made for me, those times we went to the park to play. Everything! My grandmother was not just a part of my growing up, she was the one who held it all together for me! I survived those horrible years because her love and wise words kept me.

Now she was dead. Gone! She died at 81.

My sister made no attempt to console me; not because she didn't care, but because she knew that was not what I needed.

What I needed was a good cry! I needed to let it all out! The burden, the pain, the agony! So she let me. But she sat down there on the kitchen floor with me, after tending to my wound, and she watched me cry. She watched me start the long and healing process.

****

It was five months after grandmother died, that Joe followed suit. So much for healing process! It seemed that the can of misfortunes that had been let open, was not done releasing its contents. So I stopped healing; and just resolved to absorb the blows as they hit me. Maybe healing was going to come much later. But right now, it was time to toughen up, brace up and show up!

Chapter
12

The People I Called Friends

I know you're still itching to find out what was the issue with me on the day I was rushed to the hospital in an ambulance. Yep, I've not forgotten, hahaha.

And that long lasting thing between Ken and I? Coming soon...

No dear friend, I'm not trying to keep you in suspense – though you're free to be captured in this trap, hahaha – but I'm actually trying to tell my story in such a manner that you would appreciate the very many facets of my life and its adventures.

In life, there are as many sad events as there are happy ones; there are so many things that we want them to go a certain way, but they end up not favouring us; there are mysteries just as much as there are truths and celebrations.

There are those who hate us – some for a reason and some for no just reason – and there are certainly those who love us.

I'm dedicating this chapter to those people who loved me unconditionally; who stood by me through thick and thin. These people, I call friends and I don't use this term lightly. These people showed me the true meaning of companionship and, where my family could not offer me some kinds of support, these friends of mine stepped in to do just that. I will never forget them.

Bree

Between my First and Third Grade, I had about four friends, some of whom were from church. But one of them stood out for me because she was very significant and did something remarkable for me at a time when, may be if she hadn't supported me the way she did, I probably would have been irreparably damaged psychologically.

Her name was Bree and we met when I was 7 years old. And if you're wondering what kind of support it was that Bree gave me, I'll tell you.

Now, remember that despite the fact that my family loved and supported me, they couldn't be with me all the time. There were certainly those times when they couldn't be there to shield me from racist hostility. Those were the times that I would sit or play alone, avoiding the spiky lashes that those White supremacist threw at me. Guess what? This was when Bree entered my life and made it just a little bit bearable.

Bree would come to me as I'm sitting alone and would ask to join me.

"Can I sit with you?" She asked the first time. That had taken me aback, especially as I turned to see that the person who had asked that question was a White kid. Was she mistaken? Or was she just trying to tease me?

Well, since it was a polite request and I was brought up well-mannered, I responded politely as well, "Sure." And Bree sat with me, after which both of us fell silent for some awkward seconds.

"How are you?" She asked, trying to get me to relax and open up.
"I'm fine." I answered, still unsure of her motive. "And you?"
"I'm good." She answered. A few more seconds of awkward silence. And then,

"Would you like to go play with me?" She offered ever so kindly.

"Umm...sure." I answered. What was there to lose anyway? Even if it turned out that she was just setting me up, it wouldn't be past anything I'd already faced or experienced. So why not?

And so I played with Bree that day. And another day. And yet another day. Our friendship grew and blossomed and just for the record, we were friends for about ten years! Yes! She was that good a friend! Unforgettable!

Lois

The reason I won't be able to forget Lois was the simple fact that she loved me despite my skin colour. We'd known each other right from childhood and she was always there for me despite the backlashes I received from the ugly effect of racism.

For me, the fact that she stood by me and remained my friend, regardless, simply proved to me that she genuinely cared as a good friend.

She just loved the Blacks.

Thelma

We met during our secondary school days and just like Bree, Thelma supported me in those times when I needed company most.

What was special and remarkable with my friendship with Thelma was the fact that we did those challenging teenage years together. It was good to have someone I could call a friend, who understood and wasn't judgemental.

I relished our friendship all those years and it did last till we were adults.

More about Thelma later.

Pretta

I could confidently say that Pretta was my best friend when I moved. While I had colleagues and neighbours whom I had great relationships with, I could only count Pretta as a friend.

We met after Joe passed away. She was a barrister.
I drew a lot of strength from Pretta; she was a whole pillar of strength. She was support personified!

After Joe passed and while I was ill, she was always there, bringing me things in the hospital and encouraging me all the way. Not only did she support me in her own ways, she also made other people to shower me with love and care too. While I was in the hospital, she got a lot of people to send me cards, as I was away from work.

When I got well, sweet Pretta and I became best friends, always together, hahaha.

Naomi

This was my South African friend. We also met when I moved but after a while, she went back to her country.

But that didn't stop us from remaining friends. We still talk, up until present.

Collins

And then there was Collins, who was a married man.

Hey, don't go running away with your imaginations okay? Hahaha. Collins was a married man, yes. But I was also friends with his wife.

I met Collins and his wife from one of the very many parties we attended together. Nice guy and blessed with a beautiful, friendly and supportive wife.

For a long time, we didn't see – I lost their contact; as I was sure they lost mine. We would reconnect years later!

Collins and his wife had two grown kids.

Friends from work places

I did have a bunch of people from the Gym where I worked – and other work places – who were dear to me. They kept in touch even after I stopped coming to work, and we have remained friend till date!

Chapter

13

My Illness

And now back to the part I know you'd been itching to get back to!

Remember the day I was waiting for Ken to go out on a date, but then I had to be rushed to the hospital in an ambulance? Good.

That day was the beginning of what I can only term, hell on earth because the torture I suffered thereafter, I do not even wish it on my enemies.

But prior to my date with Ken on that fateful day...

****

It started with some thickness on my skin.

Some allergies, I thought. So I didn't pay much attention to it, telling myself it would go with time and also making a mental note to watch the things I ate.

I worked in a gym; I worked out well; I was fit and healthy. So I told myself nothing was wrong with me and I moved on with my life.

Then I started to collapse!

had come back from work on this particular day. Yes, it had been a hectic day but that was what my typical day was like. It was always busy and tasking at the gym; one was practically on the move. So the tiredness I felt on this particular day was just like I'd experienced on every other day.

I had gone into the kitchen to get a plate from the kitchen cupboard suspended on the wall. Mind you, this was a routine I carried out almost every day so there was nothing new or strange.

The last thing I remembered was reaching up to get the plate. Then blankness! I blacked out and apparently collapsed on the floor, where I found myself when I had regained consciousness and became aware again of what was going on. The plate I was trying to get had landed on my head. Thank goodness I wasn't hurt.

I still didn't think there was any medical danger so I continued to go to work, continued to live my normal life. I kept telling – or rather, reassuring myself – that I was perfectly okay and my assurance was that I worked in a gym. I was healthy. I was fit. I kept reassuring myself.

Next time I collapsed, it was in a coffee shop. And again, I had blacked out and had no awareness of what was going on. All I remembered was that someone was helping me to get up.

Now let's backtrack a bit to the day I left the hospital upset because they couldn't do anything to reduce the discomfort my varicose vein was causing me. Remember? Good.

As far as I was concerned and as far as my health was concerned, this was the only medical condition I knew I had. And since it wasn't any major thing, I was okay and only needed to have it checked out once in a while.

So these collapsing episodes that were becoming unpleasantly regular were very strange to me. I was battling with making sense out of it.

One day, at work, I started to experience a seizure; my whole body was shaking – my hands and my legs too. I couldn't walk! My colleagues rushed me to the hospital in an ambulance. I was checked and dismissed after some examinations and a few prescribed medications.

For me, I still thought it was nothing serious. Maybe I didn't eat enough that day. Or maybe I was simply dehydrated – it could have been that I did not take enough water.

And then came a time when I noticed that I couldn't speak properly; something had gone wrong with my speech. You can't even begin to imagine how I felt with this new development; it was as if I was being torn apart, falling in pieces. It was one issue after another.

During this period of speech problem, I felt very weak and slept all day and night. Maybe this was to help me regain strength; or maybe that was a side-effect of the ailment, but I did sleep a great deal.

As with the earlier developments, the speech defect was rectified but it kept me wondering what could have been the cause. I did get better and even went back to work – I had to take time off work during the period I was ill.

Be it as it may, I knew something somewhere, still wasn't right. You know, as human beings, we are blessed with those things called intuition and gut. We always had those eerie feelings when awful things were looming. I think God blessed each and every one of us with that gift; whether we then decide to listen to it or not, is up to us. But we always know, or at least have that feeling.

It was because of this same gut feeling that something was still not right with me that made me to go and see a cardiologist. I just couldn't bear the suspense anymore; just couldn't keep guessing blindly.

"Your test results show that there are some changes..." the doctor started telling me.

"Changes?" I cut in, panicking. What changes was he talking about?

"Calm down, ma'am. Nothing that you can't manage."

"You sure?"

"Sure." He reassured me, "You can even go back to work."

"Oh, that's great." I responded. I thought if I could go back to work, it meant I was fit and healthy enough.

I was in and out of the hospital till the major blow struck!

****

I was supposed to go out with Ken.

There was just something that kept us together. So we were still seeing each other and going out on dates.

Maybe our relationship was just best the way it was. You know some connections are like that? The moment you tried to go beyond a certain level, things would crumble. And that proves the belief that not all relationships are meant to lead to marriage. However, my relationship with Ken lasted for 5 years.

Anyway, so I was waiting for Ken to pick me up so we could go hang out. Again, I realised that I couldn't get up. Not again!

Without wasting any time, I reached my phone and tried to reach him so he could get there sooner. I was not okay! But his number wasn't going through; I kept trying anyway.

As much as I needed help, the last thing I wanted was to attract any attention to myself. I had suffered enough embarrassment during the periods I collapsed and people had to come help me up. Not that I was ungrateful; but one still had one's dignity, you know. And while it wasn't my fault that my health was not one hundred percent, I still had my pride and didn't want to constitute public nuisance.

I tried Ken's number again; it still wasn't going through. During these periods I was trying to reach him, I would discreetly try to get up again, but most certainly couldn't. Something was terribly wrong! And I needed to get out of there fast! If anything serious was going to come out of this, I certainly didn't want it to be in public.

Finally, my call to Ken went through.

"Hello…!" I greeted in a shaky voice.
"Hi, are you okay?" He responded.
"Please where are you?" I asked anxiously.
"On my way to you. Anything wrong?"
"Yes, please try and get here faster."
"Be right there!" He replied and cut the call. I could hear the concern in his voice and I knew he was going to practically fly to me.

While I waited for Ken, I sat still, not making effort anymore to get up. I feared I could do something that would worsen the situation. So I just sat still and waited. Till Ken arrived eventually.

"What's the problem, Eve?"
"I can't get up, Ken. Something is wrong with my legs." I said, half fearfully and half embarrassed. I knew the only way I was going to get out of that place was being carried.
'Here, let me help you out." Ken said and did exactly what I knew he was going

to do. He carried me in his arms, out of the place and straight to the car.

"I need to go back home." I announced.

"Not the hospital?"

"No, I'll manage this evening."

"Okay then." He agreed and took me straight home.

When I got home, I was exhausted, drained, worn out. I could barely move or do anything. Ken stayed a bit and helped out with a few things before he finally left.

That night, I could literally hear my heart pumping! It was beating so fast and I guess that was what was sapping me of all my energy.

All night, I was laden with all sorts of thoughts? Was I going to die? Was my heart bad? Was it anything that could be treated once and for all? Was I ever going to be normal again? What did the future hold for me? Will I ever find or fall in love again? Will I ever get married? Would I have my own family? So many questions and all the answer I could hear was my heart pumping ten times more than normal.

At a point during the night, I thought I was going to pass out. I kept getting weaker and weaker and honestly, it was only miraculously that I survived the night.

Next morning, I gathered all the energy left in me to do two things.

First I called my father and explained everything to him. He mentioned he was going to come over; and then I went on to the second thing.

I called an ambulance.

****

Chapter
14

Here Comes The Storm

Let me tell you a secret – I hate hospitals!

Yeah, I know it's ironical, isn't it? The same place that is supposed to keep me alive is the same place I detest so much.

I just couldn't stand the smell, the metal instruments, the syringe, the sad look on the sick patients' faces, the nurses who were always trying to hide things from you – they said it was for your own good, hahaha – and the doctors whose face were forever expressionless. You could never tell, from facial expression, the severity or laxness of the piece of news a doctor had to share.

As I got to the hospital, the first commotion was in getting me out of the ambulance and into the hospital. As they rolled me in, other nurses and some doctors ran out to meet us and were updated about my medical records and conditions.

"Heartbeat is 180/190 at the moment..."
"...patient is extremely tired, movement is an absolute challenge..."
"Any previous medical conditions?"
"Varicose veins, thickness on the skin, patient has experienced collapsing in the..."

These exchanges went on among the nurses and the doctor as they rolled me in. All I could think of was that I wanted to go home! The last place I wanted to be in, was the hospital, ill or not!

Unfortunately, this was the only place that held the keys to the next 24 hours of my life. Of course I knew that God was up there watching; but with the way I was feeling, it looked like I was all by myself.

"Hello Eve, can you hear me?" The doctor in charge started saying, leaning forward so I could hear him. I nodded weakly.

"That's good, Eve. You are doing well." The doctor praised my effort. "I need you to know what we are about to do, okay?" My energy level was fast dwindling so all I could do was to nod and watch helplessly as they all scrambled desperately to save my life.

"First, we need to stabilize your heartbeat, okay?" The doctor informed me. I nodded.

"Is there any family member here with you?" I nodded and opened my mouth to talk but nothing came out. So I managed to mouth, "My father..."

"That's fine," The doctor acknowledged, "I understand you perfectly. Is he here?" And as if he heard us talking about him, my father walked in at that very moment "I'm her father." He announced.

By afternoon, all medical effort to put my heart back to normal had proved abortive! I was beyond exhaustion. Nevertheless, I still wanted to go home and I managed to tell them this.

"We can't let you go home ma'am."
"Why not?" I protested. "I'll be fine!" Really, Eve? I silently sneered at myself.
"We need to keep you here and monitor your progress."
"I'll be fine!" I fought weakly.

But the nurses and doctors wouldn't oblige me. So they kept me back; against my will, I must say. Hahaha.

That midnight, I was transferred to a ward. I started sweating suddenly and couldn't move again. Oh, dear!

Being that they had to leave me so they could attend to other patients, I was given a phone which was always beside me. I guess this was for emergencies or just in case I needed anything.

Which I did!

My breath was seizing; I could see myself slipping out of consciousness. I couldn't breathe! Now finding the strength to pick up the phone to call for attention was even a challenge. My whole system was weak and I just couldn't lift any limb.

Finally, I managed to reach the phone and gathered all the energy left in me to make that urgent call. And they came immediately, in fairness to them. But all I remembered saying was, "I...I...ca...can't...br...brea...breathe..." before the remaining energy in me dissipated.

Before slipping into unconsciousness, I did feel the sharp and metallic piercing of the syringe as they administered some injections to me. ***Then nothingness!***

****

Chapter
15

All Hell Is Let Loose

I woke up the next day, covered in tubes and needles!

My whole body was pierced! I lay still on the bed and the only parts of my face that could move were probably just my eyes. I had a breathing mask on my nose, and this also covered my mouth.

So I rolled my eyes sideways and there was a nurse standing there, checking my medical chart. She wasn't looking at me and since I couldn't call out, I just kept staring at her, willing her to look my way.

It worked. She looked at me and her eyes dilated in what I interpreted as both shock and pleasant surprise. But instead of coming to me, she ran out the door, shouting, "Doctor! She has come to!"

Come to? I just came to? What happened to me?

Oh, yes! I remembered. I blacked out yesterday and judging from the nurse's responses some seconds ago, I must have scared the living daylight out of every one of them! Remembering that sharp poke from the syringe, I tried to move and my whole body went into a unanimous pain frequency. Then I remembered that I was all pierced up!

Shortly, the nurse and the doctor walked back into my room and the doctor was actually smiling. Oh, yeah, I did give them a good scare yesterday night.

"Try not to move or talk, okay?" The doctor advised me softly, getting out his stethoscope to check my heartbeat. Next, he spread my eyes wide with his hands to check...I honestly didn't know what exactly he was looking for.

Since I couldn't move any part of my body, I only stared at him as indication that I understood him.

"Well, you are one lucky woman, Eve!" The doctor finally announced, when he was done with the necessary checks.
"You are, indeed!" The nurse agreed, grinning from ear to ear.
What happened? Was the question in my head but I couldn't voice it. Well, they heard me obviously, because the doctor went on to explain.

"You went into a coma, Eve. Your whole system shut down!"
For real? Me? Coma? Wow! I knew I was weak and couldn't breathe; but falling into coma? My whole system shutting down? I wondered silently.

"We had to shock you..." The doctor continued explaining.

Hang on...I knew what that was! Now I began to understand what the doctor meant when he said my whole system shut down! So they had to virtually shock me – medically though – so they could jumpstart my system again. Otherwise...

"If you hadn't been brought here yesterday, Eve, you probably wouldn't have made it..."

Hey, doctor! Let's call a spade, a spade! You mean I would have died if I hadn't gotten to the hospital when I did. Isn't it? My God!

Apparently, when my system shut down, so did my brain! And when they shocked me – thank God they did – my brain was saved. I couldn't even imagine being alive but brain dead! God forbid!

But....

The whole shocking thing lasted for about 3 minutes. Straight 180 seconds of lifelessness! Wait for it...

When they shocked me, my heart stopped! For 180 seconds – 3 whole minutes – my heart stopped pumping, stopped any form of activity. Now here was the thing; unlike the rest of my system which only shut down, my heart outright gave up!

I died!

I was dead for 3 minutes. Now I understood why the nurse was so excited! Now it was clear to me why the doctor was all smiles when he walked in. I was dead for 3 minutes! Whoof! Gone!

I could only lay there on the hospital bed, listening to all my medical progress report. I did count myself, not only lucky, but so so blessed! Despite all odds, I was still alive. That meant there was really something extraordinary God wanted to do in my life!

Ken and my father came later. By this time, the breathing mask had been removed from my nose, so at least I could talk, albeit so weakly.

The doctor came again to give more report.

He greeted my father and Ken and after he had gotten permission to go ahead with the report, to Ken's hearing, he went on to explain.

"We found out that Eve's heart is clogged." The doctor pointed out.

Oh, don't think he said this that clearly and in such a straightforward manner, hahaha. Of course he had to go round and round and in those big medical terms, till Ken had to appeal.

"So what does that mean exactly?" He was just as confused as I was. But of course my father understood, since he was a retired doctor.
"Ummm…I'm afraid there's more…" The doctor continued.
"Okay…" My father responded, trying to hold it all together. "What's that?"
"Her lungs are also clogged. This explains the difficulty in breathing and the weakness that accompanies it as a result."

My father nodded his understanding. Ken and I just listened, trying to make sense of the whole thing. What exactly was the problem here? What could have caused all these?

"And she has pneumonia." The doctor finished.

My dear friend who is reading this book and life story of mine, I was only 38 years old at this time! Where did the clogs come from? For crying out loud, I was healthy and fit; I exercised regularly and I even *taught* it! So why was there any issue concerning the heart?

I guess this was what made it so painful for me! To think that I never smoked! And here I was with a heart condition? Heart and lungs clog? Pneumonia? This was just so devastating!

"Hmmmm…" My father sighed.
"Wow…" Ken exhaled sadly.

And there was a few seconds of awkward silence. I think everybody was trying to clear their heads and think of what to say next. Really, what was there to say?

My father spoke first, "So what do we do, doctor?"

Ken leaned forward on his seat; I could imagine that he was itching to hear what the doctor had to suggest. What was the solution here?

"Well…" The doctor started saying. You could tell that he was trying to pick the words he used to break the news to us. "Here's the thing…" He paused now, again trying to compose his message in the best, possible way, "With these clogs and the pneumonia that we've traced, the truth and reality is that Eve's chances of survival are very slim…" And he left that to sink in.

I saw Ken's head fall down sadly. My dad was also obviously saddened by this awful news but he still tried to keep his cool.

For me? I was just thinking, 'So this is how I'm going to die? So I'm going to die at 38? Way younger than my mother, even!'

"So, how long are we looking at here?" My dad asked.
"Say, two to four years…" The doctor supplied.

Ken looked up at this moment and looked straight at me. I could see all the pain and agony he was going through for me and my heart reached out to him. He had been so understanding and supportive, always there to help in any way he could.

"Are there any options?" My father asked.
"Actually, yes…" The doctor replied, "She could use the defibrillator or look a maximum of 4 years to live. I'm so sorry…" He offered gently, looking at me, ". but these are the only two choices we have."

"I'll leave you now." The doctor excused himself. He knew we needed time t

More Than Just A Skin - Memoirs of Eve

assimilate the news and think about which option to go for.

"Thank you." My father said politely. This was certainly no easy pill to swallow for any of us. How could a father bear the news of his daughter's death announcement? Was that not excruciatingly painful?

And as for me, I just kept saying to myself, 'You can't die at 38, you're too young! It just wasn't a pleasant feeling *when* you were told when you would die, especially if you were still so young. As I was! Not the best of experiences to have!

****

My father and everyone else were of the opinion that I opt for the defibrillator. For them, that would, at least, keep me alive.

But Ken and I thought otherwise.

He encouraged me to have faith in God and trust that He would do His will in my life. He was of the opinion that I shouldn't use the defibrillator, but trust God. He was a good Christian and had even led me to accepting Jesus as my Lord and personal Saviour. Which I did! Few days after my health issues started.

We would pray together and join our faiths, believing that God was going to do what only He could do! Ken came regularly to see me and I must say that this was the period we really got very close!

Personally, I wasn't comfortable with opting for the defibrillator. I had asked them to show me what it looked like and when they did; plus, I saw the one man who was using it – his bed was just next to mine – I knew for sure that I didn't want to live like that!

So I told them I wasn't opting for the defibrillator. I let them know I wasn't going to depend on a machine to live! I told them that my life – whether I lived or I died - was up to God! And I continued praying; I always had a Bible next to me!

****

My friends visited me at the hospital. They all genuinely cared about me; I must say that I felt so cherished and loved.

But on the flip side, my health was deteriorating – I couldn't even talk properly. I was coughing persistently and always breaking out in sweat. It did feel like I had a stone in my heart! To say I was too weak was going to be the understatement of the century!
I couldn't shower; I couldn't get up to do the basic things other human beings did.

****

Finally, the hospital had to make me choose! It was either I opted for the defibrillator or face living for only about 4 years, max!

I had seen what the defibrillator looked like and how somebody who was using it lived; so I knew for sure it was not an option for me! With the defibrillator, I was going to be living like a robot! There were all sorts of restrictions and conditions; one of which was, that I could not go near the microwave! How absurd!

No! Certainly not! That was not the life I envisaged for myself!

"Sorry doctor," I finally responded to the doctor one day, "I am leaving my health up to God, please." I finished.

You could see that look on his face that said, I hope you know what you're doing ma'am.

"Well, Eve," he started to respond, "The thing is..." he trailed off and regarded me for a while, obviously thinking of how to let me know that by not opting for the defibrillator, I was practically signing my death certificate! "If you don't opt for the defibrillator, you have only a few years to live."

"I totally understand, doctor," I replied convincingly. My mind was made up. "I'd rather go for whatever number of years you say I have left. I will not subject myself to that machine for the rest of my life!" I finished strongly.

"I must warn you that this is a risky option you are going for..." He continued trying to make me change my mind.
"I'd rather take the risk, doctor." I insisted.
"Alright," he said as if he'd just lost a battle. "However, do note that medications are going to do very little to help." He finished.
"That's fine, doctor." I stood my ground.

Alright, I did understand the doctor's concerns. And you would too if you understood the nature of my illness. So let me try to explain it very briefly to you.

My skin was changing and my body was producing too much collagen, which made my body to become stone-like. Imagine what the inside of a stone would look like! All stiff and hard, right? Exactly!

My internal organs were affected and this contributed to the excessive sweat, difficulty in breathing, extreme weakness and fainting that I experienced regularly.

Back when I was in the Physiotherapy College, I remember hearing about this condition I had now; and I also remember them saying, then, that it was a very rare condition.

As a result of those illness conditions, my heart was affected too! And the pneumonia was still persisting.

I had injection in my belly every single day! Just to stop the blood clogging and clotting. You can imagine how numb my skin would have ended up feeling and how exhausted I must have felt! And it was really my first time of being and staying in the hospital for this elongated period of time! All through my growing up period, I was totally fine health-wise.

Anyway, I kept going back and forth, managing my health, till I was finally discharged from the hospital. I was still so weak that I couldn't even walk properly! I felt like an old woman! Hahaha.

Needless to say though, that after sometime, I had to go back to the hospital, just so that they would really ascertain that I could go back to work. So I ran some medical examinations, after which they certified me fit to work. Yet, I couldn't even go back to work, I wasn't strong enough.

Tell you what? This illness period of mine lasted about ten months! Can you beat that! Forty weeks of misery and uncertainty as to whether I was going to live or not. You don't want to know the terrible, sinking feeling!

Being that I was off work, I had to appeal to be paid for those periods of time – which I was so lucky to be granted.

I was having palpitations and after a whole year, things had not changed one bit. I was on medication, but as the hospital had warned me earlier, it wasn't really helping much. If I even as much as walked fast, I would have that palpitation.

attack! And it was usually very intense!

It was so bad that sometimes, when I walked on the street, I feared I was going to collapse because when I had those terrible palpitations, I could faint in a second!

My fear came true one day as I had the palpitation and it didn't stop as soon as I expected. So I called an ambulance and, again, found myself back in the hospital! Oh, dear!

They tried in vain to stop it the day I arrived, so I had to stay overnight. Unfortunately, it took up to two days to finally get the palpitation to stop! Thank goodness because, mentally, I really couldn't stay in the hospital anymore!

****

Back at home, and after resuming work, every time I had that palpitation, I had to rest for at least one week, after which I could then go back to my usual routines. Can you imagine living like this!

I had to regularly rest. I couldn't walk. I couldn't do anything! My body was extremely weak; I could barely move my limbs! This was the most difficult situation for me!

Friends, it is easy for me now, to write that I was in and out of hospital; and that I was weak and exhausted. But what is unbelievable here is that all this back and forth with my health, lasted for 3 whole years!

How do I begin to put into words the misery I lived through, every single second! The agony I felt every minute. The excruciating pain I suffered every passing day! It looked to me that I was never going to have any reason to smile again.

There were days I reminded myself that I had been given an option; and I asked myself why I didn't take that option and at least save myself from the pain and agony.

But then, I also reminded myself that I totally trusted God and that I had surrendered everything to him. I had resigned my faith to the Almighty God who had miraculously kept me up until then. I reminded myself that if it was His Will that I should go, then even the defibrillator would not keep me alive. But that if it was His Will that I live, then nothing was going to stop it! Not heart palpitations, not coughing, not fainting, not skin change, not heart attack. Nothing!

I still believed that God could do the undoable and change the unchangeable! I still trusted that He had the situation under control.

Little did I know the pleasant surprise God had in store for me!

More Than Just A Skin - Memoirs of Eve

Chapter
16

My Pleasant Surprise!

You're probably wondering what could be pleasant in my deteriorating condition, am I right? You are probably racking your brain now, trying to think about possible pleasant outcomes from my fatal illness. I mean, going by the doctor's prediction and projection, I only had about one year to live!

So what exactly was this surprise? And what in the world could make it a pleasant one? Well, strap on your seatbelt and let's go on this ride as I fill you in.

Friends, exactly three years after my illness started; exactly three years after I had been told I had a maximum of four years to live, the most unexpected thing happened!

I got pregnant! This was the lasting thing that happened between Ken and me. Now, you know! Hahaha.

Yes! You heard me right! At age 41, in the midst of one of the rarest illnesses in the world, I took in! I was expecting a baby! Can you even fathom this!

I was as confused and pleasantly surprised as you are! How could that have happened in the midst of all that I was going through? Honesty, getting pregnant was not even a possibility for me! I saw it as an impossibility! How could I get pregnant with my illness? Truthfully, as happy as I was, I was really concerned about what people were going to say. How would they react?

****

Of course I had to go back to the hospital so that I could get a proper medical attention. I could imagine how surprised they were going to be! Not only had I not died yet, but I was about to bring another human to this world! How ironical.

"It's too early and too risky to get pregnant, Eve." The doctor told me, without mincing words. Of course this was after he had shown surprise for the sheer miracle of my pregnancy. He had expressed how he couldn't believe this had happened, despite my medical condition; but he also had to tell me the implication. "My candid, medical and professional advice is for you to abort the baby, Eve. Your life is dire dan..."
"God forbid!" I interrupted him. Did he hear himself? Abort the pregnancy God gave me despite my condition? NEVER!
"I totally understand how you feel about this," the doctor continued, "but it's my job to let you know the risk you face if you keep the pregna..."
"I'm keeping my baby!" I interrupted again, more vehemently. "If I die, I die! But I'm certainly NOT going to kill my child!"
"Eve, please listen to me," the doctor was insisting, "You really have to..." he continued. But again, I didn't let him even as much as finish his sentence. I was having none of that!
"If God gave me a child at my age, then I'm not going to die!" I said with a note of finality. Apparently, he got my message and stance eventually; he stopped trying to convince me to abort my precious child – a gift from God to bring smile to my lips after going through hell.

****

Alright, given, I still had palpitations now and then during the course of my pregnancy. But other than that I was fine. At least, considering all I had been through.

I didn't put much weight, compared to the transforming changes other women went through during their pregnancy. I only added 7 kilos of weight. Really. Hahaha. Not obvious at all, right?

I was still as skinny as I'd been! Which is why so many people didn't even know I was pregnant, till I gave birth!

"Where did the baby come from?" some people asked.
"I had no idea you were pregnant!" some exclaimed.

Let me backtrack a bit though, and tell you about what it was like, before I delivered my precious baby...

They had told me I would have a CS – Caesarian Section – because of my health condition. I mean, that was understandable, wasn't it? Even I had started to succumb to that. Not until one of the doctors told me I could have my child normally. Do you see the mysterious and miraculous hand of God?

The reassurance that I could have my child normally got me elated and I just couldn't stop being in awe of the Sovereignty of God. He really made a way where there was no way!
But then on my due date, nothing happened. Baby wasn't forthcoming. And the doctors came again with their solutions, namely, give me some medications which were supposed to induce labour as I was overdue.

At that time, I was just too tired to argue with them, so I agreed to be given the medication. I was more concerned for my child to be born so I can hold her/him in my arms! That was all that mattered to me then.

Finally they gave me the medication, plus an epidural which, they explained, would numb the labour pain. But God was at work again! Before the epidural could get to work, I GAVE BIRTH TO MY CHILD, NATURALLY! The epidural was administered to me, only five minutes before I delivered my baby! Amazing, isn't it!

My joy knew no bounds! I held my child and gazed into her face and all I could see was the mercy of God! Our ways are, indeed, not God's ways. Everything about my pregnancy, from conception to delivery, went against man's predictions. God showed and proved that He was still God!

However, just a week after I gave birth, I developed a black clot on my leg! It was back to my ill-health! This particular black clot was to be expected anyway and here was why.

While I was pregnant, the nurses were supposed to be giving me regular injection to prevent that clot from forming. But guess what? I had vehemently refused to be injected anything during my pregnancy. You don't blame me, do you?

"I will not allow you inject anything into me while my baby is in there!" I had made clear to them. By now, they were all used to my stubbornness and didn't bother to argue with me. Instead, they had pointed out that I would have to inject myself, post birth, and while I was at home. This was because there were no available nurses who would come to my house every day to administer the injections to me.

I had to live with the realization that I had thrombosis! It was so bad that couldn't even go to the bathroom! And while you can imagine how bad the condition is in itself; I had to live with that inability to do anything for myself, for one and a half months! With my new born baby!

My leg never came back to normal; I'm still living with it even as I write this book! But hey, I've learnt to accept it and move on with life. After all, I have m daughter to take care of now! And I am on medication, tending to the condition. Life really goes on!

Alright, I am going to backtrack again and give you a little peek at what it was like, nursing my baby in my condition.

For somebody who doesn't have any health challenges, it is quite challenging nursing a newborn baby; let alone one that had terrible health conditions. Like I did!

Can you even imagine how I changed her? How I held her? Fed her? Bathed her? All of those routines. I'll tell you how I did it...

It was all on top of my bed!

Since I couldn't really walk, I had to do everything on the bed; I would roll over to carry my baby and hold her and feed her. Most times, I cried. Not out of sadness but just out of pain. Every single movement I made was excruciatingly painful. But amid the pain, I was absolutely happy holding my baby! I couldn't have traded her for anything in the world!

I couldn't go to the bathroom because I couldn't move my legs! Ken was always there to help out. He really did a lot for me. He would be the one to hold me as I dragged myself to the bathroom.

At this point, my heart had stabilized. My major challenge was the thrombosis!

And then there was a time I had the palpitation attack and it lasted for 2 whole weeks! At which point, I had to employ someone to help me, mostly with the cleaning! It was practically impossible to do anything, really.

What could I do?

You got it right! I kept moving; one day at a time. One challenge at a time. My daughter, Meg, was my joy and my all. She kept me going!

I also did read a lot about my condition online and one of the things I read as a solution was to drink a lot of water. So I did! And it did help!

I cannot tell you that I am totally healed; because I'm not! But I can tell you that I am totally ready for what life has to offer! I can tell you that I look at the positive side of life! I can tell you that I don't look like what I've been through! I can tell you that with the right attitude to life, things actually do work. Might not be perfect, but certainly a move in the growth direction.

More Than Just A Skin - Memoirs of Eve

Chapter
17

My Daughter – My life!

Talking of which – I must confess that I was very protective of Meg as she grew up. Okay, that was saying it very mildly; *I was over-protective and obsessed with her safety!*

I remember when she started going to school, oh my, I would look for very flimsy excuses to give so I could be close to or around her.

A typical instance was once, when she was going to a school field trip and I volunteered to go as an adult guide. The ulterior motive was actually to be close to her. I just couldn't bear her being so far away from me and not knowing if she was safe or not.

I could bear to leave her in school, at least that was an enclosed area; but to have her go outside the school premises, whew! I just couldn't cope with the anxiety. It was too dangerous out there! I didn't want my angel to get hurt! So I volunteered to go on the field trip, so I could keep an eye on her!

Yeah! Yeah! Yeah! I knew that was going a bit too far; and I knew this was not good for her, especially if I wanted her to grow up and be independent. But what could I do! I was just a helpless, over-protective new mother! And how could I forget all that I'd been through to have her!

I should have just been calm and trust that the God who gave her to me, was going to protect her from any harm. Maybe I was just not that strong-minded yet, hahaha.

So I started giving it a try. I started leaving Meg alone with certain people, for a couple of minutes and hours.

Once, I left her at home with Ken and went to the hospital. Of course it was the longest time in my life, those moments I was away from her! I envisaged all terrible things in life that could have happened to her. But I survived it! She was fine when I got back! Hahaha.

Next was when I left her again with Ken to go get a pusher. Another long time in my life! But again, I survived it!

And the last (and longest) time was when I left her in a party for two whole hours - which seemed more like two centuries! But you see, I was getting good at this. I was learning to let her breathe and grow. She needed to, because I was not going to be there all the time! Even if I could spare the time, again like I said, it wasn't good for her psychologically.

****

Aha! There is a juicy part of my story that I must tell...

After Ken and I stopped seeing – remember that I told you our relationship did not lead to marriage - I did meet this good and gentle guy, Brad. He was serious about having a relationship with me and he was consistent with showing his love.

As a matter of fact, he did propose to me! But honestly, at this time, I just wasn't ready for that kind of relationship. I really just wanted to concentrate on raising my daughter and being the best mother to her.

****

Motherhood is beautiful.
It is indescribable.
It made me a changed woman.

In all my health issues, I never envisaged that I would be a mother; that was the last thing on my mind. But it came and I embraced it whole-heartedly. And now that I'm a mother; all I ask myself is, "What else could I have been?"

I can't imagine my life without my precious gold, Meg! I can't imagine what my life would have been if she wasn't in it! Life would have been a mass of darkness. Total emptiness.

Meg is a delight. She is my happiness! Her voice in the house makes me light up! Am I saying she is a saint? Certainly not! As a matter of fact, she can be a handful sometimes, driving me crazy and demanding everything from me, hahaha. But I'd rather that, than be alone. Without her!

She is a grown-up now, gradually turning into a beautiful young woman. As a mother, I am elated that she is evolving; that she is becoming an individual, her own person. But then somewhere within me as well, I can't help but ponder on the reality that she will grow to not need me to dote on her anymore, hahaha.

Now my secret is out.

Yes, I do love doting on her and spoiling her with whatever I can lay my hands on. I love when she whines and demands for something. I love when we banter playfully or have one of our mother-daughter arguments. I love when we fight and I scold her to behave. I love when she pouts, sulks and gets upset with me.

And then I love when we make up! When we laugh and play with each other. When we crack jokes and laugh at silly nothings. See those moments? They are **golden** to me!

Chapter
18

Reflections

So after those years of splitting and each of us moving on, Curtis and I reconnected a couple of years back. I saw him on Facebook and we got talking. For me, that was certainly a clear proof that I had moved on. I could talk to him without any bitterness or regrets. It was totally a friendly chat.

He did tell me about his life and marriage. Of course he had separated from Heather and was alone again. According to him.

After a while, he even suggested that we meet; that I came over to where he was and that we could just sit down and talk as friends. And so I went. And we met! While I visited him, we stayed in separate hotels.

It was good to see him again after so many years. That was when I realised that I'd thought about him (more like dreamed about him) all those years. But not in regret. I think I just thought about him and wondered how he was doing; whether he was alright. It was just me thinking good thoughts for him.

On the day we met, he profusely apologized to me and dared mention that he wanted me back. Hello? Excuse Me? No way! There was not a chance in the world that I was going to go back to him. For me, I had moved on; and just because I agreed to meet him didn't mean I was yearning to get back together.

Know what? I even visited him the next year. Yes, I had completely forgiven him and moved on; we were just good friends.

****

Shocker alert!

Do you remember one of my best friends - from secondary school – Thelm.
Remember I said I was going to tell you more about her? Well, here it is.

Apparently, at some point, Thelma got involved with Curtis and they starte
seeing each other. At that point, I didn't know how close they were but I ju
learnt that they were talking and certainly more than friends.

Are you guessing now that this hurt me? Then you'd be absolutely correct!
hurt me in a way I just couldn't understand. I mean, I had split with Curtis s
many years ago and he had been with that Heather girl. So why was it hurtir
differently that Thelma and Curtis had gotten together?

In fairness to Thelma, she had mentioned to me casually, "You know Curtis is
nice person?"
"Sure, he's not intentionally bad." I responded, not that it was the best topic fi
me to talk about. But we had to chat about something.
"Yeah, I know what he did to you and all, but I think he has changed." Thelm
pointed out.
"You think?"
"Yeah, I mean, I'm sure he has learnt his lessons after all those years. He shou
be more mature now."
"I would think so." I offered and we had gone on to chat about other things.

How on earth was I to know that she was serious with Curtis! Personally, I hav
a different view about these relationship matters. There were certain peop
that I thought, by virtue of what they meant to you, you were not supposed to b
intimately involved.

More Than Just A Skin - Memoirs of Eve

I had just started talking to Curtis again; and yet he never mentioned Thelma. Let alone that they were seeing each other. So much for changing and becoming a new person!

Still, one of those holidays, I initiated that we meet as old-time friends and hang out together with some of our best friends. Curtis agreed to this and then behind me, he reached out to Thelma to invite her. And worse still, she didn't find it appropriate to tell me.

So I found out that she was coming to the get-together, invited specifically by Curtis, only when she arrived. Now you could imagine how I felt at this point! I'm hoping you can really imagine that, because I wasn't sure what or how I felt! Anger? Betrayal? Shock? Irritated? Jealous? Insulted? Slighted? I just wasn't sure at all. My emotions were all over the place!

"I didn't want to upset you, Eve," Thelma dared explain. "That was why I didn't tell you."
"What would be upsetting in telling me Curtis invited you, if there was nothing more going on?" I challenged.
"Oh, no! We're just friends. And knowing your history with him, I didn't want to start explaining anything." She offered lamely. But I knew better. More like my instinct warned me that there was more to it than just friendship.

And I could see that they were really talking. But each time I confronted Thelma, she would find one flimsy excuse or another, to give.

"Curtis and I have similar problems with our spouses, that's why we are talking." She would say.
"We are just talking, nothing else." She would insist.

Of course I didn't believe for a second that they were just friends; but I started to accept their being together. After all, I was not with Curtis anymore. They could be together, I told myself. Why not? But this was me consciously pushing aside the fact that the same Curtis had wanted me to come back to him.

"Look, Thelma," I told my friend one day, "if you really want to be with Curtis, there is nothing I can do." I finished, trying to tell myself that it was okay. I mean, we were all adults and I couldn't really tell anybody what to do.
Then, out of the blues, Curtis announced to me one day, "You know she's my woman now."

Of course I didn't have to ask who the 'she' was! My suspicion was correct all along! They had been seeing secretly; and more than just friends. But this was not even the most painful – maybe the most annoying – part of it all.

Curtis telling me about him being intimately involved with my best friend, by himself, that was a slap on my face!

I started to cry because it was like something hit me! Again, I'm not quite sure why this piece of news hurt me so badly. Maybe it was because these two people were both very close to me; and people I had, at one point or another in my life, trusted whole-heartedly. Maybe that was what hurt so bad! And to think that Curtis had wanted us to get back together? What was really his intentions? To disgrace me again? The second time?

I was so shocked that some minutes after he told me about him and Thelma, I couldn't even say anything. He had to ask me if I was still there. And if I was okay. Really? I should be okay after hearing what he had just broke to me? How insensitive could he be! How heartless he was!

****

More Than Just A Skin - Memoirs of Eve

Fast forward to my healing. That was what I needed to do immediately! I needed to brush off Curtis and his love life with Thelma. I didn't need them to come disturb the peace that I had worked so hard over the years to make with myself.

So I blocked both of them. Everywhere! Took them out of my Facebook contacts and tried to move on, even though I still couldn't believe that this was happening again. Same Curtis. He really couldn't change, could he?

In addition to blocking them I started to pray and talk to some close friends. That helped me to cope with it a bit. Talking to people was therapeutic for me and to prove how much it worked, after about twelve days, I contacted both Curtis and Thelma and told them exactly how I felt about what they did.

"I'm so sorry, Eve," Thelma apologized, "I tried to show you that I didn't want to be single anymore. You even prayed for me and wished me well in finding somebody."
"Of course I wished you well and prayed for you," I defended my action, "you're my best friend for God's sakes. That is what friends do for each other. But how was I supposed to know it was with Curtis? My ex-husband!"
"But you..." she tried defending her actions.
"Look, Thelma," I continued, making sure I poured out all that I felt so that I could be free, "I forgave what happened between Curtis and I, but I can't forget."
"Yes, I know and..."
"And then of all people to take me back to the bitter memories, you!"

I let it all out. But the more both of them kept explaining to me how they felt about each other, the more irritated I got. This healing thing was not going anywhere fast, though. Hahaha.

So I told them I needed a break. I didn't want to be a fake by pretending everything was alright. It certainly was not! They could do their thing and when I was ready,

I would get back to them. I made this clear to them.

But I knew things were never ever going to be the same again! That was not how it worked; everything just couldn't go back to the way it was before.

Now here's one unbelievable thing that happened when I indicated I needed a break; Thelma got upset! Can you imagine that! She said she didn't understand the kind of friend I was. It was all I could do not to lash out at her as I explained to her that I needed time off so I could deal with my feelings and come to terms with the new development.

Then, once again, I blanked them out! I needed my peace of mind!

****

Alright, finally when I thought I was ready, I reached out and we started talking again. But as you would guess it was never the same again! The friendship was totally different! More like, awkward.

But just so you know, we did reconnect recently – Thelma and I – and we are talking again. Yes, I did realise that there was really no need to bottle up pent up anger and bitterness; it was just too much baggage!

Besides, I had to also look inward and remind myself that I was NOT a saint after all. I did have – actually DO have - my shortcomings!

I do not want you going away from my story thinking that I did no wrong. Of course I did! I wasn't perfect, you know.

Just know that I am telling my story from my perspective and how it affected my life, both positively and negatively.

I do not hold any grudge against anybody, as I believe that everything that happened had its place in the weaving of the miracle I call my life. So, no hard feelings to anyone.

And I certainly do admit that I must have done my own fair share of mistakes. Such is life!

I am okay with Thelma as I write. We're cool.
And of course, I'm okay with Curtis. We are talking, up till date!

We're all good.

Chapter
19

At The Moment

I see myself as a complete woman! I am a complete woman!
I am not disabled! And about my health, I will keep exploring how to make tl
palpitation go away.

Maybe the world has termed it incurable. But my belief is that the God who ke
me through thick and thin would also cure me. In my research, I found out th
patients who had my condition could only last up to 10 years...

But here I am today! Diagnosed since 13 years ago! And now a proud mother!

Yes, my fingers are bloated – with the disease, I didn't get oxygen in my finge
and at a time, I couldn't even form a fist – but I still taught myself to crochet!

Yes! My Fashion is My Passion!

My health issues didn't make me sit down in one place and do nothing! I did g
after my passion and buried myself in the things I love doing.
No, I can't go to work because it's physically tasking, but I have learnt to do tl
things I can while I'm at home. Or online. But one thing I have not done is sittir
down to wallow in self-pity.

There's no way I'm abandoning my passion! I am going all the way, even if
means engaging someone to do them while I supervise or oversee. Giving up
not an option!

Speaking of which...
I found love!

I didn't give up on love; or maybe it was love that didn't give up on me. Any which way, I did find love. Again!

Which leads me to ponder...

Does **perfect love** exist? Is there really anything like, *'Love at first sight?'* Can we assume that there is a love that can last forever? Well, we all have our different stories and experiences and the answers to these ponderings would differ.

About the man that I have found and that I am with now, I did pray him into my world. He is everything I had envisaged and prayed for, as a dream husband! If I hadn't mentioned it before now, let me say it clearly: Prayers do work!

I basically prayed for my man, way before I met him; I didn't even know if he existed or not! But I prayed for his career, for his health, for his family, for everything about him!

I did visualize him before going to bed every day, to the point that I started almost feeling his presence.

In fact, I prayed for a male version of myself! Hahaha. But not in terms of physical traits or facial looks; I prayed that my man should have the same values as I have and that we would be of the same faith.

And that's exactly what God has blessed me with!

I never gave up and God didn't give up on me either. He kept directing and guiding me till He led me online one day where I met my man. Now, you must know that this is not typical of me — reaching out or talking to a man first. Oh, yes, I initiated our chat. But again, nothing about me is ordinary, wouldn't you say? God has made me so special and has also specially blessed me, immeasurably.

So there I was online, scrolling and seeing so many profiles. And something made me stop when I got to his. Surprising myself, I sent him a wink, which he responded to! And that made my day!

And that was how we started chatting. And talking.

Unfortunately, we couldn't meet immediately because of distance. We were at both ends of the world! But how I longed to see him and be in those arms I'd prayed for and envisaged. Hahaha. I really looked forward to the day we would finally meet. Which seemed like forever!

But like all long waits, it finally ended! And my man came to see me! It was simply an amazing and beautiful feeling! We talked and laughed and spent time with each other. He was everything I had prayed for!

And then boom! Reality hit! He had to go back!

I was both sad and happy at the same time. I really would have loved him to stay longer so that we could bond more. But then, it was a good thing that finally, we had met and we really liked each other. My heart hurt as he left to go back to his base; it was difficult being apart from him after I'd seen and spent fond times with him.

My man, Keith, is a good and giving man. He is always pleasantly surprising me! He is always there to listen to me and share in my world. We do talk about a lot of things and it's just a lovely, heartwarming feeling to have someone you can do this with. Especially after having gone through the valleys of the shadow of death, literally. Hahaha.

One of the heart-warming things Keith has done, that has endeared him more to my heart is that he has introduced us – my daughter and I – to his beautiful mother and sisters. My guy has introduced us to his family!

This means a lot to me, you know, considering that I don't have a mother anymore; you can relate to that, right? It's simply touching.

Keith has shown me that he values our relationship and takes it so seriously that he has let his family in on it.

Is my relationship with Keith perfect? Of course not. We do have our momentary misunderstandings, disagreements or fights; but you know what? We do talk them through! And that's what makes us know each other more. Which is a beautiful thing!

****

I have had a thousand reasons to be sad in life. But I've also had a thousand reasons to be happy and grateful. Life, they say, is not fair. When it deals you an unfavourable blow, you endure it and move on. And when it deals you a favourable one, you accept it, embrace it and make the best out of it.

That is exactly what I've done with my life – make the best out of it. While everything in it is not perfect, I try to make the most perfect moments from it.

Instead of dwelling on the negatives, I focus on the positives and think about all the possible ways I could make them even better. It's me and my mindset. It's me and my determination. It's me and my winnings. It's me and my happiness. It's me and my future. That's the way I'm looking – ahead.

As I say these final words, I do hope that you have been inspired and encouraged. I do hope that I have succeeded in igniting your fire back, if ever it had started to wane or go cold. I do hope that I have made you realise that no matter what you've been through, it can't be compared to the goodies ahead of you.

You are a strong woman.
You are capable of overcoming your challenges. What you have to do? **Believe!** Believe that situations don't tarry, no matter how terrible they appear to be.

If I focused on my health conditions, I would have missed out on the good things God brought my way and then I certainly would have failed to appreciate the people God brought to me to help me out.

In the end, God doesn't let our situations consume us. It might get to that point where it looks like He has abandoned us; but if we look closely, we would realize that those are the same moments when He is actually doing the most!

This is not a motivational speech, of course you could be motivated by my book, but the real reason I wrote this book is because I wanted to share my story as it happened to me. I wanted to share so that you could relate. And so that when I tell you to hang in there, you know I'm saying it because that's exactly what I've done all my life!

I don't see your face and I don't know how exactly you feel right now. But I do know that we've connected in a very special way, just because you've read my book and my story. I know that you have taken away one message from my story and that you've resolved to do one thing today. NOT GIVE UP!

That's right.

Giving up is not an option! You know what's acceptable? Yes, it's moving forward; it's believing; it's trusting; it's hanging in there.

I wish you all the best in what you do. And if you would like to connect with me and tell me something, a bit of your own story, I'd certainly love that. My contact details are on the next page.

From me to you, stay blessed!
Lots of Love!

CONNECT WITH THE AUTHOR

I have no doubt that there are so many young women out there who share experiences such as mine. I do know how heavy it can be, carrying those burdens and scars from our wounds.

I have let out mine by writing this book and I must tell you that it was therapeutic.

Maybe you would like to share yours?
Maybe you would to let me know how reading my own story has helped you deal with your pain?
Maybe you just want to reach out and exchange one or two words?

Absolutely!

I would like to hear from you!

Simply send me a mail at: evenaomi42@yahoo.com

Talk to you soon!

Made in the USA
Coppell, TX
26 May 2021